O is for Oval, Oswald and Osama

ALSO BY WILLIAM CLINKENBEARD

The Contemporary Lesson

*Full on the Eye: Perspectives on the World,
the Church, and the Faith* (with Ian Gilmour)

Mind the Gap: Moving between Pulpit and Pew

All Published by The Bavelaw Press

O IS FOR OVAL, OSWALD AND OSAMA

A Novel

by

William Clinkenbeard

iUniverse, Inc.
New York Lincoln Shanghai

O is for Oval, Oswald and Osama

iUniverse books may be ordered through booksellers or by contacting:

iUniverse
2021 Pine Lake Road, Suite 100
Lincoln, NE 68512
www.iuniverse.com
1-800-Authors (1-800-288-4677)

ISBN-13: 978-0-595-36911-9 (pbk)
ISBN-13: 978-0-595-81323-0 (ebk)
ISBN-10: 0-595-36911-1 (pbk)
ISBN-10: 0-595-81323-2 (ebk)

Printed in the United States of America

To Janette, who as we lay reading on the beach in Borneo, responded to my complaint about a lightweight book I was reading with: 'Well, why don't *you* write one then?'
And to Robert, Helen and John

ACKNOWLEDGEMENTS

A number or people read this book in part or in whole and made very helpful corrections, comments and criticisms. They include Ian and Ann Renton, Ian Gilmour, Ian and Pat Brady, Bill and Linda Armstrong, John and Lesley Clinkenbeard and several members of the Forthwrite Writers Group. I am especially grateful to my wife Janette, both for spurring me on and for making constructive comments along the way. It wouldn't have been attempted without her encouragement.

Taken from *My Utmost for His Highest* by Oswald Chambers, edited by James Reiman, [Copywright]1992 by Oswald Chambers Publications Assn., Ltd., and used by permission of Discovery House Publishers, Box 3566, Grand Rapids, MI 49501. All rights reserved.

...there is no historical reality, whether it be church or government, whether it be the reason of wise men or specialists, which is not involved in the flux and relativity of human existence; which is not subject to error or sin, and which is not tempted to exaggerate its errors and sins when they are made immune to criticism.

—Reinhold Niebuhr

CHAPTER 1

▼

The receptionist took his card, glanced at it very briefly and looked up at him wearing a puzzled expression. 'Freelance Theologian?' she said, 'What does that mean?'

'A theologian is someone who thinks about religion,' he answered. He had planned to add "systematically" to the sentence but changed his mind when he saw the couldn't-really-care-less look on her face. She was in her early thirties, a sharp-featured blonde in a tartan jacket. She was sitting behind a desk in the premises of the Clan Caledonia Export Company. He had also wanted to say, 'Theology used to be the queen of the sciences, and it is only lately that people like you have become so ignorant about it.' That might have shaken her out of her boredom. But, of course, he didn't say any such thing. He had been invited here to talk about some work, and so he was even more courteous than normal. The receptionist handed back his card and directed him with a casual wave of the hand towards a leather couch in the corner of the room. 'Mr. McCord will be with you shortly,' she said.

The office of the Clan Caledonia Export Company was on Bernard Street in Leith, the ancient port city that had been dragged kicking and screaming into the bounds of the city of Edinburgh. The people of Leith had never quite forgiven Edinburgh for the theft of their independence. Lane had parked in Constitution Street and crossed the road in front of a statue of Robert Burns. He studied the piece as he waited for the lights to change. Burns seemed to be looking up the road towards Edinburgh, and Lane wondered why. Had the city fathers turned his head that way just to spite the Leithers? There must be a story here, but he didn't have the time to pursue it just now. He found the right numbers on the front of a three-story stone building boasting a semi-circular front. Most of the premises along here had well-polished brass plaques at the entrance, but Caledonia Clan apparently could only stretch to an off-white plastic job with black letters. Their office was wedged in alongside an odd assortment of take-away places, estate agents, a bookmaker, and a Chinese medicine and healthcare shop. He couldn't decide whether this part of the city was on its way up or down. From all appearances that morning it was hovering uncertainly between the two possibilities. Officially, Leith was coming up, with expensive new waterfront housing, a multitude of up-market restaurants lining the shore and an Ocean Terminal designed by Terence Conran. But when he had been walking along the street from his parking place, Lane hadn't thought it looked like it was on the way up. There were surely more dodgy-looking pubs per capita than anywhere else in Scotland, the stone-fronted buildings were brownish-yellow tinted black from the years of exposure to coal smoke and car exhausts, and the Ocean Terminal, he had heard, couldn't even take ocean-going ships. Perhaps some day Leith would actually begin to look renewed.

Davis Lane sat down on the couch and rehearsed the reason he had come here. He had received an invitation from a Robert McCord of Clan Caledonia, who said he might have a proposition for a free-lance theologian. Since Lane didn't get many business propositions these days, he agreed without much hesitation. On the surface, however, he couldn't see what he might have to offer to a company that exported Scottish paraphernalia. Lane shifted on the couch in order to study the room more carefully. Several tables pushed against the walls featured kilts made up in various tartans, a huge variety of sporrans, and piles of tartan rugs. Glass display cases held a large collection of sgian dubhs and a range of silver and gem jewelry. The place would be a treasure chest for Scottish Country Dancers. Hanging on two walls were clan crests and several styles of bagpipes. Shelves holding thick arch-lever files marked "Clan Tartans" lined a third wall. Lane found himself giving an involuntary sigh as he settled deeper into the leather. He never knew how to regard all this stuff. As an American he could see the interest it held for his fellow countrymen who prided themselves on their real or imagined Scottish heritage. He knew about all the American Caledonia Societies and their clan gatherings, particularly in the South. But as someone who had lived in this country for most of his life it was all a little artificial and wearisome. The number of weddings he had taken where the groom and best man appeared in highland gear that didn't fit or was badly marked, and the kilts he had seen being worn back to front…he could have written a book. His cynicism had been deepened by the number of Scots he knew who flew all over the world to speak at

Burn's Suppers and the like. Scottish romanticism was deeply etched with a commercial interest: *Have Kilt, will Travel.*

A door opened in the corner of the room and a tall, slight figure strode through and headed his way. 'Hi, Mr. Lane, I'm Robert McCord. Good to meet you and thanks for coming. Please come in.' McCord shook his hand firmly, gripped his elbow and steered him through to a back room. He motioned Lane into a chair, moved behind his desk and sat down. He was wearing a jacket and kilt, the complete outfit, but he clearly wasn't a Scot. Lane reckoned from the accent that McCord also was an American.

'I can see what you are thinking,' McCord said, adjusting his bow tie with a smile, 'but it goes with the job. If you're in the business of exporting all these things you really need to use them yourself.'

'I suppose so,' said Lane, 'but I can tell by the accent that you're an American, somewhere from the eastern part of the country, maybe Maryland or Virginia. Don't you feel a little...' McCord interrupted him: 'A little like a fraud? Yes, sometimes. But it's good for business, and you actually get to like the kilt. It will travel anywhere and suit any occasion.' Lane only smiled and nodded, noting that McCord had not said where he was from. It was unusual for an American not to identify his origins. Many people in the States wore a badge to work indicating that they were from Iowa or Nebraska or Michigan. What was this need for a geographical identity? Lane looked around the room. It was pretty functional: a filing cabinet, two telephones, an expensive-looking pc on the desk and several photographs on the wall. The remainder of the desktop was clear except for a manila file on the pad.

'I'm glad that you could meet with us Mr. Lane. I'm hoping that we can come to an arrangement. By the way, would you like a coffee?'

Davis Lane shook his head. 'No, thanks, I had a cup not that long ago.' It wasn't true, but it was a habit he had formed during his years in the parish ministry. You made pastoral calls on people and they sometimes asked you if you wanted tea or coffee. But they always took so long fiddling around in the kitchen that in the intervening time you could have made several more calls or even mentally composed a sermon. So it had been a convenient phrase, but was clearly no longer appropriate to his new life. He was always being reminded of how much we are creatures of habit.

'No problem coming in,' Lane replied, 'but I don't quite see what I can do for you, Mr. McCord. From what I see, you obviously market all these things in the States, but I can't imagine what that has to do with me. I'm really a theologian.'

'I appreciate what you are saying', McCord said, 'but there is a lot more than meets the eye here. We do much more than send kilts and tartans and pipes to Georgia and Alabama. It is a fabulous business, by the way. We didn't anticipate that it would be as successful as it is. We now have a rapidly growing demand for tartan products in the States. The latest product on offer is a map of the clans. It's selling like hotcakes in the States. The idea is that you find the location of your clan on the map, travel over here to visit the old homeland and have a few drams on the whisky trail to celebrate your heritage. And of course, once you've done that you buy the map of tartans and discover the appropriate tartan to wear. We've also got clan key rings, clan coasters, clan paperweights, and clan fridge magnets. It's a great business. We can't produce enough of all these things to satisfy the demand. It does wonders for tourism and stimulates the Scottish economy. You should take a look at our website.' McCord was grinning broadly, showing a set of very even, very white teeth.

'I took the liberty of doing that already,' said Lane, 'and it is impressive. I can imagine how appealing it would be to the people who believe that their roots are in Scotland. They find what they want and order it online. You must have a lot of hits on your site because every other person I talk to in the States claims to have some connection with Scotland.'

McCord nodded absent-mindedly, picked up the manila folder from the desk, and leaned back in his chair. He opened it and studied it intently in silence for a moment. 'Could we talk about you now, Mr. Lane? As I understand it, you come originally from the Midwest; you have a postgraduate degree in theology; you were a minister in the Presbyterian Church in the States and then a minister of the Church of Scotland. You retired about a year ago?'

'You've got it about right' Lane said, 'but I'm surprised that you know so much about me.' McCord said nothing, so he continued. 'I didn't really want to retire. I just needed to do something different, have a change from the parish.' He was aware that once again he was trying to distance himself from the ranks of the old and retired. The trouble was that as a minister you are so pigeonholed that it is nearly impossible to do that. Other professional people seemed to be able to change what they do, but not ministers. It bothered him that in the eyes of society a minister who wants to do something else must either be incompetent or have lost his faith. 'But the only alternative was to be a hospital chaplain or an administrator in church headquarters,' Lane continued. 'I didn't like the idea of either, so I decided to become a freelance theologian, which is nearly unheard of. People usually laugh when I tell them what I do. There are freelance journalists and photographers and who knows what else, but not freelance theologians.'

'So what does that mean?' asked McCord, who wasn't laughing. 'How do you do theology on your own? Does it mean that you analyze religion for people? Are you a theological critic? That's the way that we look at it, but tell me if I'm wrong.'

'No,' answered Lane, wondering what the "we" meant. 'That's pretty well it. Most of my work so far has been writing educational-type courses for use in churches or helping ministers to lead programmes about worship or church organization. But what I'm really about is enabling people to think clearly about their faith, or about their non-faith as far as that is concerned. The trouble is that we live in such a secular age that there isn't a lot of interest. The market for theology is nothing like the tartan market.'

McCord leaned forwards and put the folder back on his desk. 'Well, we are interested. We're looking for someone like you. May I call you "Davis", by the way?' He went on without pausing for a reply. 'Davis, just between you and me, tartan is not the only thing we export. We also specialize in what could be called info-export or information sharing between here and the States. As you know, the world has become a very small place. The ripples that start here and head across the pond may be waves by the time they get there, and vice versa. The bottom line—and it's delicately drawn—is that there are important agencies and people who find it useful to have contacts here in order to use them to gain access to an understanding of what is happening in this country. There is nothing strange about this. After all, there is a special relationship between the UK and the States.'

Lane smiled 'Yes, he said, 'there is a special relationship, but it's a peculiar one. I've been watching it for over thirty years. What amuses me is that while the Brits get anxious about losing this relationship every so often, they also exhibit a lot of anti-American feelings. They want their holidays in Florida and their films from Hollywood and the money that comes with the tourists, but they don't want to be tainted with anything bad from America. If you listen to the media then everything that's bad comes from the States—the ruination of the English language, drugs, and the domination of the world by international conglomerates. But the next minute they're falling over themselves to discover how many British films have won an Oscar. There is something peculiar about that.'

McCord nodded but seemed momentarily lost in thought. In the silence Lane studied the view through the window behind the desk. A derelict building under demolition filled half of the scene. A rusty crane was swinging a ball against the far brick wall. In the other half of the scene the gray waters of the Firth of Forth were rolling in. It was now darker outside and raining. McCord, rising abruptly from his chair, suddenly blocked the little light filtering through the window.

'You're right of course,' McCord said, 'but that's no longer relevant to the current state of play. Let me try to spell out our thinking for you a little better. The war with Iraq is officially over as you know, but the internal violence is actually increasing. Tensions are running very high throughout the country. You will know all about the history of hostage-taking and brutal murders, I'm sure. No matter what the politicians say, it isn't clear what is going to happen in the future. Iraq may well become a very fertile seedbed for growing terrorists. The United States and Britain are far more vulnerable than they realize. America seems to be hated throughout the Middle East, and that hatred is rubbing off on Britain. Right across the world there is increasing conflict between Christianity and Islam. There are masses of people pressing to be independent of western influence. You've seen the pent-up anger expressing itself on television. It's a very dangerous situation. We want you to analyze this situation and predict what kind of relationship between the Muslim Middle East and the Christian West there might be on down the line.'

Lane sat upright and then leaned forward in his chair. 'Mr. McCord, I think you are wasting your time talking to me. I have some expertise in theology and ethics, but I've spent most of my life as a parish minister in the Church of Scotland. There are lots of guys, academic types, who can talk to you about relations between Christianity and Islam. There are experts on terrorism now, something unheard of twenty-five years ago. Tune in any morning to the BBC and you will hear them. Go to Edinburgh University, any university and you'll find people better qualified than me.'

McCord smiled at this, once again displaying his even, very white teeth. He came round to the front of the desk, perched on it and leaned forward until he was a foot from Lane's head. He lowered his voice.

'We knew that you would say that. But listen Davis, you have certain other skills and experiences which appeal to us. You have lived both here and in the States. You have the ability to move around freely here, you have a lot of contacts, and—McCord put both hands lightly on Lane's shoulders—there are several aspects of this work that we can't talk about here. All this is very much confidential. Trust me until I can tell you more.'

'I still can't see...' but McCord interrupted once again: 'The other factor, the one we haven't mentioned yet is money. For a starter, there is five thousand pounds in it, and if things progress as we hope, more. What do you say? Let's meet somewhere for lunch. You suggest a place, somewhere lively and noisy, where we can speak freely. What about Thursday? Are you free on Thursday?'

Lane thought for a moment, trying to distinguish between the counsel of his better judgment and the man's persuasiveness. He was trying to think of a good restaurant at the same time. 'What about Harry's Bar in the west end? A lot of business types go there for lunch. The food's OK too.'

'Great,' said McCord, 'see you at Harry's Bar on Thursday, say at half-past-twelve.'

'OK,' Lane answered. 'But let me ask you this. When you say 'We', who do you mean?'

'I'll explain over lunch', McCord said.

The outer room was empty and quiet as Lane left, apart for the blonde staring intently at her monitor.

CHAPTER 2

▼

The rain was bouncing violently off the pavement as Davis Lane left the premises of Clan Caledonia Export Company and turned into Constitution Street. He ran to the car trying his best to avoid the deepening puddles and wondering why he had ever agreed to a further meeting. This job was not his cup of tea, and there was something very odd about it. Who were the "we" in Clan Caledonia Export, and why the air of secrecy? He probably should have turned McCord down, but in truth, he was curious, and he really did need money.

He found the PT Cruiser and behold—there was no parking ticket on the windscreen! Thanks be to God for small miracles. You could never tell about parking in Edinburgh any more. The traffic wardens were like vultures, circling around vulnerable vehicles, just waiting to swoop. He wondered how they managed to be invisible one minute and then materialize round your car the next. The funny thing was that when they did materialize it was in boxy style uniforms and caps that were always several sizes too large. But no ticket this time. Maybe they were sheltering from the rain.

At the lights at Ferry Road he put on a CD: Garth and *Ain't goin' down til the sun comes up*. It wouldn't be that way tonight. He was tired. By the time he got home and had something to eat, he would be ready to go down. As always, the PT Cruiser attracted attention from other drivers, even in the driving rain. It was pure thirty's, Al Capone style. He still felt somewhat self-conscious about driving the car, but so what? It was a mile away from the normal, boring body style, comfortable and spacey inside, and that's what he liked in a car. Katriona hadn't been that enthusiastic, but he had talked her into it, stressing its practical points and playing down its radical looks. This afternoon it seemed more appropriate than ever as he drove away from the strange meeting on Bernard Street. The recitation of his conversation with McCord and the style of the car conspired to induce an air of intrigue. He had done absolutely nothing untoward, yet he felt vaguely guilty. It made it worse when other drivers studied the car and then stared hard at its driver.

Ferry Road was horrendous at this time in the afternoon. He should have thought of that when he made the appointment with McCord. The traffic would be solid past Warriston Crematorium and Golden Acre and Crewe Toll and on west. When he finally got to the traffic lights at Barnton, Lane put on Willie Nelson—*On the road again, just can't wait to get on the road again*—. This A90 to the Forth Road Bridge was hardly the kind of road the song referred to, not the kind of open road he liked and that he felt free on. But it was better than the traffic jam he'd just come through. And it was better than he had experienced once, several years ago. He and Katriona had been heading towards the bridge. They had been to some event or other—he couldn't remember—but they had had to go in separate cars. Katriona had gone straight from work in her old MX5, and he'd gone from home. But once they got on the bridge road, just about here, they found it bumper-to-bumper and not moving. The MX5 was right behind him, but they hadn't had their mobile phones and couldn't communicate with each other. They literally inched along. The large electronic sign on the highway simply read *Forth Road Bridge Closed*. Lots of help that. He thought that these new signs were supposed to provide you with more information. All they did was to tell you what you already knew: *Mirror, Signal, Manoeuvre*. Either that or gave you moralistic advice: *Don't use mobile phones whilst driving*. Where else in the English-speaking world did people still use *whilst*, he wondered? After at least forty-five minutes the bridge was in sight. But it was clear that all vehicles were being directed up the slip road towards the roundabout. When Lane got to the roundabout there were two policewomen speaking to each driver. He put down the window. The policewoman said, 'Are you going north, sir?' Lane said, 'Yes, to Inverkeithing'. She said, 'I'm sorry, sir, the bridge is closed. You'll need to go via the Kincardine Bridge.' Lane sighed. This was a real nuisance. The Kincardine Bridge was miles upriver. He stuck his head out the window. 'Can you tell me why the bridge is closed?' The policewoman answered, 'Yes, Sir. Because someone is trying to jump off it, Sir.' A jumper. He felt ashamed. Those *Sirs* had a certain edge to them. Here he was complaining about a few extra miles while someone was contemplating the Big Jump. If only jumpers could know how much damage they would do to their loved ones, how they would cripple them forever. Suicide meant that there was never an opportunity for relationship repair, for an explanation or even conversation. He'd seen it all before.

Nevertheless, sandwiched in a stream of traffic, the two cars headed off towards Kincardine. It was another hour before they reached home and fell into bed. The following day, when Lane was coming back across the bridge again, he asked at the tollbooth, 'Last night the bridge was closed because you had a jumper. Did he jump?' The man in the booth answered, 'Nope.' That was all. Just 'Nope'. The jumper was probably home drinking a cup of tea and being comforted while the Lanes were still winding their way home on the back roads from Kincardine Bridge. And now in torrential rain on the bridge, Willie was going strong—

> *On the road again,*
> *Goin' places that I've never been*
> *Seein' things I may never see again.*

CHAPTER 3

▼

The next morning Lane was up later than normal. It hadn't been a good night. He had had a nightmare sometime in the middle of it. In the dream he was sitting in his own lounge looking down at the blue carpet. Then he had spotted something on the carpet. On closer inspection it looked like one of the pieces of jewelry he'd seen at the Clan Caledonia Company the previous day—an attractive silver Celtic brooch into which was set an amber stone. But in his dream the brooch had turned into a large spider that began crawling towards him on the carpet. And then there was another and another and finally an army of moving spiders, heading relentlessly towards him. The whole carpet seemed to be alive and shifting under his feet. He had tried to stamp on the spiders with his foot but it made no difference to their advance. Fortunately, the violence of his kicking motion had awakened him. After that he had lain awake thinking about the dream and trying to figure out what the assignment he had been offered by Clan Caledonian was really about. A Scottish export company wishing to employ a freelance theologian to provide them with some kind of suspect information: it wasn't making sense. Eventually, he had dozed off for a while.

He drew back the curtains and stood at the bedroom window, hands on the sill, looking out over the Firth of Forth. The tide was in and the waters calm. It was going to be a nice day, fresher because of the rain. It had even cleared some of the dust out of the air. He couldn't figure out why there was always so much dust on the furniture here. He suspected that it came from the whinstone quarry just across Inverkeithing Bay. There was always smoke or dust rising from the crusher, along with the occasional explosion. He had promised Katriona that he

would keep the house beautifully tidy, and now he could see dust on every surface. Lane sighed; he hated dusting. It could wait until later.

His eye wandered down the hillside from the quarry to the breaker's yard.
Alongside a solitary crane there were huge piles of twisted and rusting metalwork.
Every morning he studied the yard to see if the two small but rather neat, rusting
vessels moored at the dock were still intact. It pained him to imagine that they
were slated to end their life at this yard, having travelled the great seas of the
world. For their crews they must surely have been homes away from home, travelling vaults locking up a multitude of shared experiences. The past was so easily
dismantled, hoisted up and hauled off as refuse. He was beginning to think that
the only real constant in life besides God was change itself. The one thing you
could count on was that everything around you—the people, the landscape, the
customs and values—would change every day. But even this was not completely
true, for he also recognized that the rate of change itself was changing—ascending daily on a technological escalator.

Lane had heard that the breaker's yard across the way had been famous
because of the great ships it had handled in the past. Even the Mauritania had
been taken apart here. It was said that up and down the Fife coast you could still
find pieces of its furniture in hotels and bars. Lane hadn't explored much yet, but
it would be strange to find yourself eating at the captain's table in some Fife
hotel. However, now the yard seemed to be a declining business, for he could
never see any much activity around the dockside. Studying the vista from his
window, he suddenly realized that in truth the town they lived in was surrounded
by waste. On the south side it was the piles of rusting steel from the breaker's
yard and the jumbled rolls of paper at the paper mill on the near side of the bay.
On the north side it was the wagonloads of wrecked cars in Inverkeithing rail
yard. Cars were apparently brought here from all over the country after they had
been written off. The town was virtually surrounded by stacks of waste; was this a
paradigm for the future? Nothing like living in the middle of a midden.

However, that was enough aimless meditation for the moment. He would
need to get a move on, for there was plenty to do today if he was going to take
this job. Some shopping and housekeeping were required at the very least, and
most of all, he needed a haircut.

Lane shaved, showered and dressed and then had a quick breakfast. He had
decided that he could walk into town today. It would save the hassle of parking.
The Lanes had found a detached villa just beyond a row of slightly rundown ter-
raced houses near to where Inverkeithing petered out down by the bay. The road
stopped here, dead-ending at Fife Coastal Path. Theoretically, you could walk or

cycle all the way from here to St Andrews. He hadn't had time to do that yet, nor had he had much time to work on the house. They had purchased a place here because property was so much more reasonable than in Edinburgh. The way things were going in the city you needed to be seriously rich even to buy a one-bedroom apartment. But the property craze had not yet infected this part of Fife. Their house was near the water, which appealed to Katriona, and yet there was a fast rail link to the city. They could be in the centre of Edinburgh in twenty minutes. The property was in need of some modernization, as the estate agent's ad had said. He was getting to that, but it was slow going. So far he had only painted the lounge and the hall. The bedrooms on the first floor looked out over an overgrown field that ran down to the path. It wasn't a particularly attractive view, but at least you could see the bridges.

Lane locked the front door and walked down to the road. He hadn't expected the chill in the air, but perhaps it would help to clear his head. If you turned left here you went alongside the SMM Warehouse, which boasted a pier running out into the bay. Lane had seen stacks of timber, commercial lawnmowers and electric caddy carts being unloaded. Further along, where you were really on a part of the Coastal Path, you soon came to a disused quarry, whose dark waters lapped a sheer wall of mottled brown stone. A steel link fence ran round the quarry, but it was ripped and open at several points. Lane always thought this would be a dangerous place for children. Jutting out into the water of the bay were the rusted remains of a steel pier. Sections of it were missing, and barbed wire had been stretched across the gaps to bar access to anyone brave or foolish enough to attempt to climb it. Lane supposed that in the dim and distant past it had been used for loading stone carved from out of the quarry. People sometimes came down here just to hang about or to try out their motorbikes or to do who knows what else. Further along the path the landscape became more attractive as you approached Dalgety Bay. There were metal gates across the path and an occasional seat.

He appreciated now that their house was a little isolated and the outlook slightly gloomy, but it was home, and it was *their* house. Having lived in a manse for years, they appreciated actually owning a house, like most everyone else he knew. No more church property committees coming round for an annual inspection which never led to any work being done; no more asking permission to paint a room himself; no more gas bills to heat a house too large and too draughty. On the other hand, like other ordinary mortals, they now had to maintain the property and pay the council tax themselves, which was a good reason to pursue this job.

If you turned right and headed uphill towards the town, you passed a small park and a variety of styles of houses. The houses were a mixture of old and new, council and private properties. On the other side of the park was an Elizabethan-style pub standing on its own in an unlikely spot, but apparently still doing business. Further up the hill were several small garage-type businesses. Once you crossed over the railway line and got past the church, you emerged on the main street. Inverkeithing, he knew, had an old and venerable history dating from the twelfth century. It was a royal burgh and had been a customs port. For all the history, however, it seemed a bit down at the heel. The main street was a kind of lazy L shape, running from west to northeast. It certainly had more than its share of pubs and bakery shops. Lane couldn't figure out why there were so many bakery shops. Were the good people of the town especially keen on pies and morning rolls? There was the usual collection of takeaways, betting shops and tired coffee shops, but one didn't get much sense of life in the place. There were two exceptions: there was a small hardware shop near the end of the street. It was superb. You could barely get in the door, for the rest of the shop space was crammed with useful, household articles. For a small shop, it seemed to have everything. They even still had screws and bolts and hinges in boxes! The kind of shrink-wrapped packs that either provided you with too many or two few was unknown in this store. Even better, the ladies behind the counter actually knew what hinges and brackets and mortice locks were. Ask them for a two-inch spread bolt and they reached into the drawer and pulled it out for you. Across from the hardware shop there was also a good cycle shop. It was a prime location for a cycle shop, for the town was on the national cycle network. It must have helped, for every time he walked past, the place seemed to have customers in it. Lane had bought their own bikes there after they moved into the place. A wee guy who hardly seemed out of high school had told him more about cycles than he really wanted to know. Reaching the roundabout in the middle of Main Street already, he'd once again, how quickly you could get there from the house.

Still, for all the rationality of their movement here, the Lanes had not appreciated that the Kingdom of Fife was a different world. Geographically, It was only a dozen miles from the city, but mentally and culturally it seemed a thousand miles away. Both Edinburghers and Fifers thought of the place "across the water" as a distant and foreign world. The estuary was a mental border as much as a watery one. Lane still found this amazing and he couldn't get acclimatized to it. The bridge, whether it was the rail or the road bridge, didn't only connect two pieces of land; it connected two very different ways of thinking and being. This fact was driven home to him when he had reason to consult a specialist at the local hospital. When Lane had described his symptoms, the consultant had looked up sharply from his notes.

'Where are you from?' he asked bluntly.

'I live in Inverkeithing,' Lane answered.

'But you're not from Inverkeithing, are you?'

'No,' Lane answered. 'I'm an American.'

'That's what I thought. I can understand you.'

'Sorry, what do you mean?' Lane had asked.

'I'm originally from up north, so I have difficulties here in Fife,' the consultant said. 'I can't understand most of my patients. It's the Fife accent.'

Lane had experienced the same thing himself in speaking to local people. He really didn't want to run down his new locale, but if the accent in the Kingdom of God were like that in the Kingdom of Fife, he would never be able to converse with the saints. He crossed the road and headed west to the fringe of the town. It was there he would find Melvin.

CHAPTER 4

▼

Melvin's Mobile Barber Shop was parked in its usual place just outside the town centre. When Lane first discovered the business he had carefully noted in the back of his diary the usual days Melvin came to Inverkeithing on his way round West Fife: Inverkeithing, Dalgety Bay, Aberdour, Burntisland and Kinghorn. The barbershop was in fact an old bus that had been converted to suit a travelling barber. Towards rear back of the bus were the barber's chair and the neat compartments where Melvin kept the tools of his trade: scissors, clippers, combs, brush and mirror. At the front were several rows of seats for waiting customers. A magazine rack held the day's tabloid newspapers and old magazines. A red and white striped pole slowly rotated in the front windscreen. Melvin kept the cover at the back of the bus open with the engine running to power his electric tools and to provide a continuous airflow. Lane actually preferred the mobile shop. It was more like the barbershops of old; it had a more masculine feel to it. There were plenty of hairdressers in the town, but most of the shops were unisex these days. The hairdressers always seemed to be teen-aged blondes who were bored by their work and couldn't be bothered to venture into the realms of meaningful conversation. Melvin was different. Melvin had opinions and was unguarded in his expression of them. Once you were imprisoned in the chair and under the nylon sheet you were a suitable recipient. Not that it was a monologue; Melvin appreciated conversation. He could listen as well as speak.

The other thing that appealed to Lane was the barbershop's mobility. In travelling around the Kingdom of Fife, the barber picked up gossip and news from all over. Melvin's customers came from all classes: tradesmen, professions, ex-miners and the unemployed. Women and children came for their haircuts as well. Moreover, Melvin didn't only get the town locals as customers, but various travellers as well. Indeed, Lane was amused to see a UPS van driving off just as he arrived, the driver waving to Melvin through his open door. It was always easier to park where the bus was than to find a parking place in town. Lane kept kidding Melvin by asking him why he hadn't called his mobile barbershop "Hair Today, Gone Tomorrow."

Melvin was short and stocky and always wore a short-sleeved white shirt with a colourful bow tie. He wore a handlebar moustache and his hair, apart from the round bald spot in the middle, always appeared long and unruly. Lane sometimes kidded him: 'It's time you got a haircut, Melvin.' The answer was always the same. 'Nobody wants to cut my hair, Mr. Lane. They don't like my business.' Lane supposed that it was true. The town salons probably did not appreciate a mobile barber coming in to siphon off a share of their business.

Melvin threw the cloth over Lane's shoulders and tucked it in round his neck. He fixed his customer with dark, piercing eyes. 'What do you want today, Mr. Lane?' he asked. The question and the answer were always the same. 'Short all over, please Melvin, and taper the neck.' This opening exchange between them was now becoming a ritual.

Melvin's old boxer, sleeping in his basket near the wheel arch, emitted a sigh, as if to say, 'Not the same old haircut yet again.' Lane had never seen this dog awake, but it sometimes sighed deeply in its sleep or made yipping noises to accompany its dreams. He supposed it was chasing a rabbit or courting a bitch. He suddenly recalled his own dream last night and sighed inwardly.

Melvin started snipping. He was left-handed and the fastest cutter Lane had ever seen. 'How's your family Melvin?' asked Lane. He knew that the barber had four children, two of which were teen-agers.

'Oh, they're all right,' Melvin answered, somewhat wearily. 'But they all have so much to do. My other work is running a taxi service for them, and they hate being taken anywhere in this bus. I had to buy a used car just to ferry them places.'

'I sympathize,' Lane responded. 'Couldn't you just turn off the barber's pole when you take them?' Lane grinned at Melvin and got a blank look back.

"So what's happening around Fife? Lane asked, raising his voice to compete with the noise of the engine and the music from Kingdom FM. 'What are people talking about?'

'Football, mostly,' said Melvin. 'People are following Celtic. They like to see some competition for Rangers, even if they aren't Celtic fans. There needs to be more competition in the league. And there's a lot of talk about the price of property. Everyone thinks it's ridiculous. There are ordinary houses in the backwoods of Fife going from over two hundred thousand pounds. It's all people from the outside buying these places, mostly the English. They've made money down south and sold their property there. Then they come up here for the good life. But the Fifers can't afford these houses. It makes people angry. Then the guys from the Black Watch are shipping back from Iraq and coming in for a haircut. But they are very quiet except for making small talk. They don't say anything about the war. I don't even ask them anymore.'

Do they say anything about their experience in an Islamic culture?' Lane asked. 'It surely must have been the first time for most of the guys.'

'Nope. They don't say much about religion, except for the fact that they were always being woken up by the calls to worship. These people are fanatics.'

'Well they are just serious about their faith, unlike most people in this country,' Lane responded. In the full flow of conversation Melvin seldom gave any facial expression of emotion. But Lane had noted that he spoke with his scissors; there was a direct relationship between what Melvin felt and the speed of the scissors. The snipping was now going faster. Lane always worried about his ears at such a moment.

'Oh, I know they're serious,' Melvin said, 'you can see that from the TV—the way they pray on their mats and the way they carry on in the streets. But what's it all for? What difference does it make? They believe in God or Allah, but God doesn't do anything. Here is all this violence. People are being killed. Saddam was killing them before the war. Hostages are being taken and then murdered. What does God do? He could stop it, but does he? No way. All these people being bombed, he does nothing. What kind of God is that?'

'Yes, It really is awful,' Lane said. 'The violence is so destructive and yet so pointless. But I think we often have the wrong image of God. We think of God as all-powerful, as a kind of big guy in the sky who can just reach down and fix things. He's not like that.'

Melvin was finishing up on Lane's neck now, making fast upward strokes with the electric trimmer. He pushed his head first to the right and then to the left. He looked at Lane in the mirror. 'What about the top?' he said. 'Do you want some off the top?'

'Yes, please,' Lane answered.

Melvin began lifting Lane's hair with his comb. Taking two fingers of hair with his right hand and cutting it with his left, looking a little agitated and snipping at an even faster rate.

'So why shouldn't we think of God like that?' Melvin asked. 'I grew up as a Catholic and my mother was pretty religious. She made us all go to church every week. I went to classes with the priest. I was taught that God had plenty of power and that he could do anything. I thought that he made everything and that he was supposed to care for people. I mean, he made us and all. Isn't he supposed to be able to put things right? Why should we believe in him if he doesn't make the world better?'

'Yes, that's what I learned when I was growing up too,' Lane said. 'But that was in Sunday School. We get these Sunday School images of God in our heads and it is hard to get them out. Maybe God is limited. Maybe he is loving but not all-powerful. I believe that God loves us but that he can't do everything. He's involved in his creation, so he can't just step outside of it to fix things.'

Melvin suddenly stopped snipping and gave a baffled look to Lane in the mirror. 'I don't follow you,' he said. 'If he's God, surely he can do everything. What is the point of believing in a God who can't do anything? In this kind of world, with people killing each other and starving, he should sort it out.'

'Oh, I know, I know,' Lane answered. 'I totally agree with you that there is a lot wrong with the world. 'But I think it's a question of how God works. He really works through people in ordinary ways. He doesn't do miracles all the time. Most people have a totally wrong view of God. They still think of him as the old man with a beard up in the heavens who can reach down and fix things here on earth. So when he doesn't fix things up for them they reject him. They wind up rejecting something that was never real in the first place. Look, Melvin, suppose I said to you that I didn't like watching soccer football because the players never had a huddle to decide on the play, never threw a forward pass, and never picked up the ball to run with it. What would you say to me?'

Melvin paused once again and stared incredulously at Lane in the mirror, his eyes widening darkly. For a moment he appeared to be speechless. 'That's crazy,' he said finally. 'That's ridiculous saying that, Mr. Lane. If you said that to me I would say that you don't know anything about the game at all. Zero understanding."

'Exactly,' said Lane. "And you would be absolutely right. And in the same way lots of people reject Christianity because their basic understanding is pathetic, almost zero. They've been given a completely false picture of God from their childhood or even from the newspapers, and because it doesn't square with reality, they have rejected it. Even today in the space age, if you mention the word "God" to people, they think "up", as if there were a heaven up there with God sitting in it. It's a concept from another age, but we have to have a more sophisticated idea now. You try it, sometime, Melvin. You mention the word "God" to a customer in the chair and watch him in the mirror. He'll look up.'

'That's not a good idea for me, Mr. Lane. I want people to look down so I can cut their hair. I have to keep pushing heads down as it is. Anyway, If I mention God to them while they're in this chair getting a haircut, they'll think I'm crazy, Mr. Lane. And they might never come back again.' A faint smile appeared on Melvin's face.

Melvin raised his arms and resumed his work. He was finding up the odd strand to deal with here and there. 'It's kind of hard to bring in God when you're cutting people's hair. You know what I mean? It's not like talking football or something.'

Melvin finished tidying up Lane's hair and reached for the mirror.

'OK, that's it,' he said finally, holding the mirror behind Lane's head. 'Is that OK for you?'

'It's fine Melvin. It looks a lot better. Thanks for the conversation as well. It's good to talk to you.' Lane handed over a five-pound note and waited. Melvin exercised his cash box and went to hand back the change, but Lane shook his head.

'Oh, thanks,' said Melvin. This was another of their little rituals. Lane always gave him a little tip and Melvin always acted surprised, as if it were the first time.

As Lane reached for his jacket and headed for the door, he heard Melvin's voice.

'So where is he then?' asked Melvin, motioning to his next client to come to the chair.

Lane hesitated and looked back as he reached for his jacket. 'Where is who?'

'God,' replied Melvin. 'You said he wasn't up there in heaven. So where is he?'

'He's here, in the world, Melvin, beside us and around us. It makes more sense to think of God as being down than it does up. He's like the ground we stand on…. but we'll talk some more about it the next time,' said Lane.

Melvin was already working on the next customer, who was looking from one man to the other with the most peculiar expression on his face. The barber didn't bother to turn around. 'O.K. See you.' he said. 'Take care now.'

The sky had turned darker since Lane had entered the shop. The air was chilly around his newly trimmed head, and there were spots of rain appearing on the pavement. He hurried up Main Street towards home. He hadn't really received much news from the mobile barber today. Moreover, he felt that he had confused Melvin by the little theological conversation. But hell, that was his job. He was a freelance theologian. Anyway, he suspected that Melvin enjoyed it as much as he did.

Lane went to the supermarket and bought enough groceries to last for the better part of the week ahead: some fruit and cold meat and bread and a few oven-ready meals. Last of all he swung along the wine and spirits aisle and bought a bottle of Lagavulin. 'This is extravagant,' he thought, 'but I'll probably need it in the days ahead and I'll be judicious with it.' Once at home, he accomplished the last item on his list for the day by sending an email to Katriona. Where was she now, he asked, and how was it going? He told her that he had a new project. He told her that he missed her.

CHAPTER 5

▼

Harry's Bar was in the West End of Edinburgh, tucked in behind Charlotte Square and just off Queensferry Street. Apart from a small neon sign and the menu posted on the wrought iron railing outside, you would hardly know it was there. Lane liked the way that the place startled you. It was the contrast between the rather obscure, tradesmen's-like entrance in a quiet lane, and the crowded interior of the restaurant itself. You went down a worn flight of steps from the pavement, opened two nondescript doors and a surprisingly large room opened out before you. A series of yellow and blue stained-glass lights ran over the bar in a dogleg to the left. Facing you at the very back, several tall stained-glass windows looked down on a raised platform offering tables which afforded greater privacy. Electric blue walls surrounded the dimly lit dining area. Coming in from a largely deserted street, you discovered a space overflowing with noise and people, mostly dark-suited guys in their thirties. Harry's was a popular place for lunch for the financial types who worked around Charlotte Square. It was also close to the Church of Scotland Headquarters in George Street, but Lane had never seen anyone from the church offices here—too far beyond the pale, he guessed.

Robert McCord was standing at the bar and waved to Lane as he came through the door. No kilt today, instead a grey suit, button-down blue shirt and red and blue striped tie with a raincoat over his arm. He greeted Lane with the same enthusiasm he had displayed in his office two days ago: a strong handshake and a clasp on the elbow. Lane was aware once again of the engaging grin and very white teeth.

'Davis,' he said, 'what a great place. I like it. How are you doing?'

'I'm fine,' Lane replied. 'How are you?'

'Great,' said 'McCord. 'Let me get you a drink. Then we'll get a table and talk.' Lane asked for a pint. The waitress led them to a table in the back corner and they sat down.

'I hope you've been thinking seriously about our proposition, Davis,' McCord said.

'I have,' Lane answered, 'but there are things that don't add up here. You said that you wanted me to look at the relationship between Islam and Christianity as it has developed after the war. You said that there were groups who would find that kind of information helpful. But a) there really are other people better informed than me about this subject, and b) What does this have to do with a company which exports Scottish tourist stuff?'

'Good questions,' said McCord, looking down intently at the menu. 'Let's order and then I'll spell it out for you.'

They ordered. McCord studied their fellow diners for a while and then took an extra long swig of his beer. 'I know that on the surface, the connection between tartan and terrorism isn't very obvious. But as I said to you, there is another aspect to what we do, and that's why I felt it would be better to talk about it somewhere else. It is slightly delicate.' McCord rolled his hand from side to side slowly to underline *delicate*. We do want you to look at the kind of dynamic that is emerging between the West and the Middle East, and that includes the whole business of terrorism. America is attracting hatred from nearly everywhere at the moment, and yet most Americans don't even know that yet. The whole middle part of the country between the east and west coasts is covered by a cloud of 'don't know, don't care.' This is what makes the situation so dangerous. We would like someone from outside the culture to spell out why there is so much hatred, but we don't want it to be an academic exercise. That kind of stuff is two for a penny, easy to come by, as you said yourself. We're interested in you because you're a theologian who has his feet on the ground. You know what ordinary people are saying and thinking. You have access to the real world, and we want the insights that come from someone in the real world. You know now that there are people in Britain who are committed to the radical cause. The London bombings proved that. You know about the bombings in Bali and Madrid and everything that has gone on in Iraq. Some of the terrorists have already been arrested—the administration is saying seventy-five percent, but I think that is questionable. Some of them are being monitored; but probably the majority of people in this camp are unknown. People like to think of the terrorists as foreigners, but most now are probably home grown. We'd like to get some theological perspective on this thing.'

Lane put down his glass and came in more sharply than he intended: 'I'm sorry, but so far this still doesn't make any sense. You're speaking in such general terms that there is no handle to grab onto. What is it you want me to do? What has this to do with exporting kilts, for God's sake? I can't see any connection. It sounds more like a covert operation, and by the way, who do you mean when you talk about *we*?'

'Well,' McCord said, leaning back in his chair and slowly exhaling, 'it is. Don't worry about the *we*. It's only force of habit. I'm only referring to the company.'

Lane was about to respond when the waitress arrived with their order. She set the plates down and asked if there was anything else they wanted.

'We'd like some tomato sauce, please,' McCord said, 'but could you leave it with us for a while?' He smiled a charming smile and said to Lane as she turned, 'I can't understand restaurants here. You ask for ketchup and it's only a temporary loan. They try to take it away from you after five minutes.'

After the waitress brought the tomato sauce, McCord took a pen and business card out of his jacket pocket and wrote a number on it and handed it to Lane. 'Let me try to make things clearer,' he suggested. 'But this is strictly confidential, absolutely between you and me. Is that agreed?'

Lane nodded.

'Have you ever been to Virginia?' McCord asked.

'Only once,' said Lane, 'to Richmond. I spent some time in the library at Union Seminary.'

'Well,' said McCord, 'if you've been to Virginia or probably even if you haven't, you know about Langley and what goes on there. If you were to phone the Langley code and then this number, you would understand who we are and what we are about.'

'I see,' said Lane, staring at the card. He felt the hairs slowly rising on his neck.

'What I've been talking about just now—the relations between the West and the Middle East, the rise and the future of terrorism, etc.—that's just a convenient label to attach to the real project. It allows you to explain what you would be doing for public consumption. When people ask you what you're up to, you can say that you are doing a theological analysis of the roots of terrorism, or something like that.'

Lane held up his fork in order to signal a question, but McCord put up his hand in return. 'Let me come to it. As I said, it is a little delicate.' He looked around the room and then moved closer over the table.

'The fact is,' McCord said, 'We have certain anxieties about people in high places.'

'Like who?' asked Lane.

'Well,' said McCord, 'there are several. But you may know that the president engages in very disciplined reading each day. This seems to be very important to him. He reads a book written by a Scottish Preacher—name Oswald Chambers. It's called *My Utmost for his Highest*.

Lane was nodding. He had read an article to this effect in *The Scotsman*.

'Probably,' said McCord, 'there is nothing especially unusual in all this. After all, the man is obviously very committed to the faith. But there are some people—I can't name them for you—some people close to the President who feel that this attention to Oswald Chambers is both obsessive and interesting. They wonder where it is going to lead him. They wonder how it might pre-dispose him to act in certain situations. We think that they also think that his interest in the book might present opportunities. The Company shares some of these concerns, but for a different reason. I can't say more than that. I scanned the book and it actually seems pretty bland to me. I can't figure out why the president and thousands of other people are so obsessed by it. But then, I'm not a theologian.'

'Are you saying,' said Lane, 'that the President could be a dangerous man?'

'Oh no,' said McCord, smiling yet again, 'I couldn't possibly say that. All I'm saying is that we think it would be useful to have someone study the material, maybe check out the history of this guy Chambers and then write an analysis. That's why we've come to you. Surely you can see why you are suited for the job. You are a good theologian but also a low profile one, no offense intended. If we approached someone in a university department, it would be all over the tabloids the next day. There is no way we could ask some well-known academic to do this.' Lane, thinking of the Scottish theologians he knew, wondered who would fall into that category.

McCord dipped a chip into the tomato sauce, held it up to his mouth and looked intently at Lane. 'You're not eating,' he said. 'Is there something wrong with your order?'

'It's not that,' said Lane. 'I'm just thinking that what you're asking me to do sounds like international espionage, and that's not my line.'

'No, that's taking it too far,' said McCord, shaking his head from side to side. 'There is nothing illegal here, nothing untoward. There isn't any law against making a theological critique of a book for an agency is there? By the way, I haven't talked about money yet. I wanted to be sure that you were happy with this project. Over and above what I promised you before there will be fifteen thousand, pounds that is, not dollars. When you finish your research and write it up and we have a final chat, the money goes into your account. OK?'

'Hold on, I've not said I'll do this yet,' said Lane. 'I need to think about this.'

The two men ate in silence for several minutes. Lane was preoccupied with what he was being asked to do, and McCord seemed to understand that.

Lane was the one who broke the silence. 'I don't know if I really want to get involved in international espionage,' he offered. 'I don't have any expertise in this sort of thing.'

'Look, we're confident that you can handle this, 'McCord said. 'This is just a theological exercise, a critique of a book. There is nothing illegal in it. Surely it's the sort of project that appeals to you, and I know that you could use some extra income. You said yourself that there isn't much work for a freelance theologian. I'll be right beside you at every step.'

'Tell me what it is that the agency are trying to achieve in this,' Lane said, studying McCord's face hard for some expression that might further his comprehension.

'It's nothing that specific yet,' McCord answered. 'What you probably don't know is that relations between the administration and the agency have been a little rocky for a while. We've been being accused of trying to undermine the President. That isn't true. We just want to pursue our proper role here without being politically exploited. We just think that your work could help us clarify the picture, give us a sharper image of how his mind works. Now, what do you say? Will you give it a go?'

Lane thought for a minute and finally answered. 'I guess so,' he said, with some hesitation.

'Good.' McCord reached over to grab his hand and shake it. 'Then there are two other things which I should mention to you,' McCord said. 'First, don't get in touch with us. We'll get in touch with you after a while, when we think you'll have some preliminary results. Second, I have to tell you that there are other interested parties. This reflects something that the ordinary man on the street hasn't come to terms with yet, but needs to, and you need to as well. It's a different world now, since 9/11. Al Qaeda is everywhere, and I mean everywhere. You're used to thinking of Edinburgh as a safe fortress, the castle on its rock rising above the violence of the world, tattoos on the esplanade, and so forth. It maybe was like that in the past. I don't know because I haven't been here that long. But I do know that the city wasn't even touched by the trouble in Ulster. It's different now. Better get used to seeing cops with submachine guns on the streets because the terrorists have personnel even here in this city. And it's not just terrorists. The security services are piling their teams into every major city in the world. Every government needs to know what's going on. You think MI5 isn't interested in what the president might do? Think again. You think that Mossad isn't here, listening in? Think again. They don't want their hands tied over Palestine. And there are other people involved, perhaps not identified, but digging to see what they can find out. All I'm saying is, Davis, watch your step.'

McCord called the waitress over to ask for the bill. Lane sat silently, still debating the issues with himself while the other man settled up. They got up and walked to the door. McCord paused halfway up the steps to the pavement outside Harry's. He shook hands with Lane again and said simply, 'Hey, don't look so grim. You'll be fine. I'll be in touch. Good luck and take care.'

Lane wandered along Queensferry Street in a daze. When he got to the P.T. Cruiser, there was a ticket on the windscreen. He hadn't even thought about checking the time in the last hour. He pulled the ticket off the windscreen and shoved it into his pocket. He could hardly be bothered, for the fact was he was trembling. All the way home he kept going over his conversation with McCord. 'Did I hear him right? Is this a CIA operation? Is the President of the United States of America thought to be a dangerous man? Who all is involved in this business? What on earth am I letting myself in for?' The chill he had felt earlier had now settled in firmly. He was cold and anxious, but he had to admit it to himself, a little exhilarated as well.

At home that night, after a dram and his oven-ready lasagne, Lane settled down at the keyboard of his pc. After a quick search he found that there was indeed a website for the CIA, and within it was the telephone number McCord had written down. Then he went into Amazon on the web. He ordered a book: *My Utmost for His Highest*. In his mailbox there was at long last an email from Katriona. He would need to respond, but what should he tell her? Finally, he ticked the reply button on Katriona's email. He had better let her in on what was happening. The question was, how much should he let her know?

CHAPTER 6

▼

Katriona was in Guatemala serving as a voluntary social worker. She had committed herself to go for one year in order to help one of the social work agencies acting in Guatemala establish the policies and procedures of their developing programme. Most of their social workers were fairly young, so Katriona's wide-ranging experience in Scotland was regarded as very valuable. It provided them with some badly needed mature leadership. Having worked for more than twenty years in several of Edinburgh's more deprived areas, she thought she had seen most everything there was to see about the nitty-gritty of life. But now, the job was turning out to be very demanding, and she found that in fact she hadn't yet seen everything. What happened on the streets of Guatemala City shocked even her. But she was clearly enjoying it, at least judging from the emails she had sent. This year was her way of doing what she liked but in a new and very different context.

Katriona had arranged a one-year leave of absence from the department, but during that year she would receive no usable income. So financially, the one-year commitment would prove difficult for the Lanes. They would just about be able to manage, but only with the help of some of his lump sum retirement money and some of her savings. It would be tight, but Lane had encouraged her to go. She, like him, needed some kind of change in her existence. Once you got in a rut, the rut began to enjoy and insist upon your company. You had to have a new project now and then, and if it didn't come to you, you had to invent it. Lane had decided years ago that regular re-invention was a personal necessity for everyone. The social work organisation would fly her out to Guatemala City and back at the end of the year, but it could not afford her airfare back to the UK mid-term. Lane hoped he could fly out to see her, but it was a costly exercise. This job might make it possible—maybe for Christmas?

Still, there was now the question of how much to tell her. If he said he was involved in some sort of covert operation for the CIA she would be worried, assuming that she believed it in the first place. The best solution was simply to tell her that he was doing some writing as background information for the advertising of Clan Caledonia products. It sounded ludicrous, but she knew about the American interest in anything Scottish. She might not be able to ascertain any logical connection between that and theology, but at least she would not worry. He could now genuinely look forward to seeing her before too long. The house was empty and the days seemed endless without her.

Some background work on Oswald Chambers might prove helpful. Lane typed *Oswald Chambers* into the Google box. He was astonished to find that there were 26,500 references to the name. There was no way he could check out all of these. However, a scan of the first one hundred revealed that most of the references were to the book itself. Very little new information there. But he did learn several important things. It seemed that *My Utmost for His Highest* was one of the most widely used devotional books in the world. One of the sites claimed that next to the Bible it was the most used devotional text. He had no idea it was so popular. And it was clear from the websites coming up that it had been translated into German, and French and Spanish and who knows what else? Next, he found that by going into one website you could get the daily reading from Chambers' book. He wondered if the President did that. Did the man who inhabited the Oval Office sit down at his desk and go online every day? Probably not. He also learned that there appeared to be very little in the way of any theological critique of Chambers' work among the websites. So either the work was beyond criticism, which he doubted, or it wasn't worthy of serious analysis. He would have to see.

The book arrived from Amazon two days later. Lane got to work that same evening, settling down with it, a dram and a CD. Since he was on the trail of a Texan this evening, he thought that the Bob Wills Cowboy Band might be appropriate. Why not focus on Texas? He started off with *Deep in the Heart of Texas*. When the music started coming through the speakers he was glad to be alone. He smiled to himself because of the images it brought to mind. Katriona would have given him a hard stare and marched out of the room. She hated it and couldn't understand why he seemed to enjoy it. He asked himself once again why he liked some of this country and western when a lot of it was corny. What was it that appealed to him? He guessed that there were three things he could say if someone were ever to ask him.

First, at least this music was honest. It dealt with the things that really happened to people: falling in and out of love, getting married and divorced, suffering pain, death, and loss. These were genuine aspects of life. People went through these things, even if they didn't talk about it a lot, especially in Scotland. Lots of other music was superficial in its content. Pop, which he heard only by tuning accident these days, could be ridiculous. These video singles were pure romantic fantasy. And even opera could be silly when you thought about the underlying story in the libretto. At least country and western had a real life grittiness to it that he respected.

Secondly, Lane had decided that as an American, he was a westerner. It had, strangely enough, taken him fifty years to come to that conclusion. He had lived in the east, but it wasn't him—too uptight and nitpicking. He had never been comfortable in the time he had spent in New England and Virginia. No, he was too laid back. He liked the big blue skies arching over him and the large landscape of the west. He like open spaces where you could see for miles and no one tried to hem you in.

The stars at night are big and bright,
Deep in the heart of Texas
The prairie sky is wide and high,
Deep in the heart of Texas

If Glaswegians were a race different from Edinburghers and the two places were only forty miles apart, then surely westerners could be a race apart from easterners when the two regions were thousands of miles apart. The cowboy music underlined a profoundly different approach to life.

And finally, he had to admit that he probably liked this music because it wasn't terribly fashionable in this country. Oh, there was no doubt that it was popular with a certain section of people, but they were in the minority. It wasn't that he counted himself in that camp, but rather that being fashionable and politically correct irritated him to the hilt. People, even very intelligent people, didn't appreciate how much they were driven by fashion: what they wore, what they watched and listened to, what they said at dinner parties and what they believed. Especially what they believed. They had written off Christianity because it wasn't in fashion. But if some incoherent form of spiritually was featured in the Sunday Supplement, they would buy that lock, stock, and barrel. On the radio the other day he'd heard a woman telling about how she had decided to become a witch. Her daughter wanted to be one too! What was the world coming to? Country and Western served him as a tool to prod and prick the herd mentality.

But he had to get down to the book. The introduction provided a short biography of Oswald Chambers. Chambers, he learned, was born in Scotland in 1874. He went to the Royal College of Art in London and then to Edinburgh University. During a preaching ministry he met and later married Gertrude Hobbs, whom he called "Biddy". Together, they founded a Bible Training College in London. It was Biddy, who as an expert in shorthand took meticulous notes of Chambers' lectures and sermons. In 1915, during the First World War, Chambers volunteered to work with the YMCA as a chaplain to the Australian and New Zealand troops in Egypt. It was there that Chambers died of complications resulting from an appendectomy. It was reported that out of their great respect for Chambers, one hundred men escorted the gun carriage bearing his coffin. When Biddy returned to England she began transcribing her notes of her husband's lectures, and these became the basis of the book. Lane learned to his amazement that the book *My Utmost to His Highest* had sold over two million copies in the United States, and that after the president's commitment to the book had been noted, its sales increased even faster.

This work by Oswald Chambers was intended to be devotional rather than doctrinal. It was simply distillations of lectures given at his Bible Training College. Nevertheless, it was—like everything in life—theological. Lane believed firmly that everyone did theology; whether they realized it or not. Everyone did theology; they either did it well or badly. Their approach to life in the world either expressed a view of God, man and the nature of things that was faithful to scripture and experience, or it didn't. The people who dismissed theology as an abstract and redundant exercise were simply kidding themselves. Everyone had some view of the world, unless they were merely surfing on its surface. In that case their approach was too superficial to be taken seriously. If people wanted to exhaust the gift of life by merely surfing along, that was their problem. He knew that you couldn't really compare Chambers' work with that of the great theologians, but he still had a theology, and Lane would soon find out how adequate it was. He found himself beginning to warm to the task.

The book was meant to be read as an aid to daily devotions, having one page devoted to each day of the year. There was a text from the Old or New Testament at the top of the page along with a title for the theme of the day. Chambers would begin by quoting a sentence of the text and then use it to propound some spiritual advice. But in doing this he might depart quite markedly from the rest of the text or the context. Sometimes other texts were brought at random to support the advice. For example, the text for January 28 was a passage from St John's Gospel about Thomas's doubt in the resurrection of Jesus. Thomas says, "My Lord and my God." But Chambers then goes on to bring in John 4 and Acts 1. The bottom line is not about Jesus' resurrection, but about doing battle for God. We are not sent to do battle for God, but to be used by God in His battles. Chambers posed the question: Are we more devoted to service than we are to Jesus Christ himself? What, Lane wondered, had happened to the resurrection?

In the devotions for January 16, Chambers' text was Genesis 15:12, about Abraham falling into a deep sleep. During his sleep he hears from God about the future enslavement of Israel and their exodus from Egypt, as well as about his own old age. But Chambers then goes on to cite three other passages, and the bottom line is about having confidence in God alone: "As soon as God becomes real to us, people pale by comparison, becoming shadows of reality. Nothing that other saints do or say can ever upset the one who is built on God." So already in the middle of January, Lane thought, we have been counselled by Chambers to be supremely self-assured and thus to be ready to be used in battle for God. This was getting interesting. It looked like the President might find this counsel very congenial. After another thirty pages of reading and marking, plus another CD and another small dram, Lane went to bed. He had made a start, but there was a long way to go. Even a little bit of Oswald went a long way.

CHAPTER 7

▼

The sky the next morning was bright blue, promising some warmth for a change. At Hound Point in the Forth the sun danced delicately on the water around two tugs maneuvering a large tanker into place. The vessels docked here to facilitate crude oil transfers from onshore storage tanks. Lane was impressed at the patience of the tug crews in handling these huge vessels in all weather conditions. All the larger ships were piloted up the tricky estuary by Forth Port pilots, skirting around the Isle of May, Bass Rock, and Inchcolm Island. These guys must surely have some stories to tell, and some day he would like to hear them. Far beyond the south shore, the sunlight glinted off a plane coming in to land at the airport. There seemed to be a steady stream of air traffic these days, with a plane either taking off or landing about every minute. One of the flight paths was right over his house, and he watched a second aircraft bank and head southwest, its vapour trail dissolving in the sky.

He closeted himself in the study and began serious work on the book. He started by marking relevant sentences and making notes in the margin. The language and style of Chambers' writing was old fashioned, making reading difficult. After several tedious hours, he recognized that a break was required. He would have to do something different for a while to stimulate his mind. The grass hadn't been cut in well over a week. Maybe that would wake him up as well as provide some much-needed exercise.

After only several passes over what could only roughly be called the *lawn* Lane stopped to empty the grass collector. Closing the lid of the bio-bin, he became aware of a voice from next-door calling his name. Alison, his neighbour was waving to him over the fence. He put the grass collector down and walked over. She was smiling and wearing tight blue jeans. If there was one item of feminine apparel that moved Lane it was tight blue jeans. Alison leaned on the fence clutching secateurs and garden gloves.

'Good Morning,' Davis, she said, shading her eyes from the sun.

'Morning Alison,' he replied. 'How are you?'

'I'm fine,' she said. 'I haven't seen you for ages. Are you well?'

'Yes, I'm fine,' he said. Alison must have been in her early fifties, a widow. Her husband Neil had died suddenly—a heart attack—just before Davis and Katriona had moved in. They had tried to be helpful to her, talking with her at length on several occasions to encourage the grieving process. They had both seen so much grief in their professions that listening came naturally. Neil's sudden demise hadn't proved easy for Alison to deal with. Her only daughter was down south and couldn't get back often. The house and garden were now really too much for her over and above her part-time job at the library. Lane had volunteered to help out on several occasions, repairing the gate and cutting the grass for her when she was away from home. He studied her now to see if she seemed down or needed him to do some other job for her, but she appeared to be at ease and cheerful enough.

'How is Katriona? Have you heard from her?' she asked.

'Yeah,' she's OK', said Davis. 'They are really working her hard. She seems to have meetings every day—typical social worker—you know. She's getting to know Guatemala City pretty well from what I can see. I think she is really enjoying it.'

'And how are you managing on your own?' asked Alison.

'I'm OK. I have a project that I just started the other day. It's kind of tedious though, and I needed to get out of the study for a while. I thought I would cut the grass.'

'You'll have to take a break now and then, Davis,' said Alison. 'Katriona wouldn't want you to go at it too hard. She told me to keep an eye on you, you know.'

'She did?' Davis replied.

'Yes, I promised her I would check up on you from time to time. Now look, I bet that you haven't been making proper meals for yourself. Why not come over here and let me make you a meal? What about tomorrow night?'

Davis hesitated. Would this be a wise move? He had so much to do, and he wasn't sure he felt like taking on any more grief at the moment. People didn't know what happened in this process. You listened carefully to people, trying your best to share their troubles, and eventually the grief actually transferred in part to the listener. You found yourself carrying an additional emotional burden. Over and above Lane's reluctance to take on more grief, he appreciated that both of them were on their own at the moment and probably a bit vulnerable. But how could he refuse Alison without giving offense? Anyway, Katriona had told him not to overdo it. He would need to make time to relax.

'That would be very nice. Are you sure?' he said.

'I'm sure,' Alison replied. 'I'll see you tomorrow night, say about half-seven? And you can tell me about your new project.' She returned to her pruning.

He had to admit that the idea of a home-cooked meal was appealing, at least as long as someone else cooked it. Still, Lane viewed tomorrow evening with some trepidation. Alison was a warm and attractive woman, and he was lonely. He was finally beginning to appreciate that fact. He would just have to handle it. Would Katriona approve of this encounter? Still, if she had asked Alison to look after him…no, that was wishful thinking. Stop worrying about it; get back to the grass.

The rest of the day was spent getting deeper into the book. He was up to the devotion for March 20, and it was becoming clearer as to where this was heading. Lane was discovering the key words for Chambers' theological thinking: words like *holiness* and *surrender*. The main concern seemed to be with the growth in personal holiness of the believer. Traditional theology had always termed this *sanctification*, which meant growing in faith. Clearly for Chambers, what went on outside the person was not as important as what was going on inside. In this particular piece he found a paragraph that could turn out to be crucial for his analysis of Chambers' theology. The devotions for that day were entitled "Friendship with God", and the given text was Genesis, Chapter 18, verse 17: *Shall I hide from Abraham what I am doing…?* Chambers argued that this passage from Genesis brought out the delights of a true friendship with God. This is what followed:

> *This friendship means being so intimately in touch with God that you never even need to ask Him to show you His will. It is evidence of a level of intimacy which confirms that you are nearing the final stage of your discipline in the life of faith. When you have a right-standing relationship with God, you have a life of freedom, liberty, and delight; you are God's will. And all of your commonsense decisions are actually His will for you, unless you sense a feeling of restraint brought on by a check in your spirit. You are free to make decisions in the light of a perfect and delightful friendship with God, knowing that if your decisions are wrong He will lovingly produce that sense of restraint. Once He does, you must stop immediately.*

The paragraph set alarm bells ringing in Lane's head. Chambers was saying that there were stages in the life of faith—nothing particularly radical there. But at the final stage the believer gained an intimacy with God that permitted freedom, liberty and delight. This meant in turn that in such a stage all the decisions of the believer reflected the will of God. So if the believer was convinced that he was intimate with God, he could be sure that his decisions and actions were really those of God himself. A *feeling of restraint* would be unlikely to present itself in such a situation. This was a bold and potentially dangerous proposition. What if a believer as powerful as the President of the United States actually bought this argument? Lane felt the little chill run down his spine once again.

He was also beginning to see how the president would appreciate this work. He knew that Alcoholics Anonymous had often recommended this book, and he had read that the man had been very dependent on alcohol. The book's emphasis on discipline, on overcoming bad habits, on being saved from sin, and on personal progress towards holiness would be appealing to anyone trying to overcome a dependence on alcohol. But if, in such a powerful figure, the sense of being saved and of being intimate with God produced an absolute self-confidence that refused to acknowledge the advice or counsel of others, it could be devastating for the country and even for the world.

There was a curious anomaly here. The thrust of Chambers' argument was leading to an individualistic personal holiness. What really mattered in the end for him was the individual's personal relationship with God. This in a real sense was for him the Christian's *work*—to win others by appearing holy. Even the problems encountered by others were not to be sympathetically viewed by the believer. Chambers was actually suggesting that such problems might well be sent by God to force the person to turn to Jesus Christ. So, for example, Chambers would probably argue that Alison's suffering was sent to her by God in order to turn her towards Christ. Moreover, he would say that Lane ought to make her grief worse in order to further the process. Such a theological position was abhorrent to him. It made God into a cruel manipulator. Moreover, in all of this, the realities of the world outside would surely recede and become less important. So the bottom line for most of the saved would mean gradual withdrawal from the world. But, for a true believer with real power—such as presidential power—the bottom line could be radical involvement in the world. A person absolutely convinced of his righteousness might exercise a power unfettered by anyone or anything else. Even close advisers would not stand much of a chance over and against such intimacy with God. The only thing that might limit presidential power would be a desire for political survival. Lane could now begin to see why various groups—whoever they were—might want to exploit such a possibility. He put the book down, feeling more than a little shaken.

CHAPTER 8

The next day Lane was absorbed in the book from early morning to late afternoon, stopping only to break for coffee and have some lunch. He was once again reading, marking relevant passages, and making notes. The overall drift of Chambers' approach was becoming clear, but it wasn't getting less tedious. He also took some time out to do some electronic banking. The five thousand pounds that McCord had promised had indeed been transferred into his account, no name specified, only a reference number. The payment cheered him up; it provided a healthy boost to their bank account. At half-past five he went up to the supermarket and bought a bottle of wine and some flowers to take to Alison. Just after six he went to have a shower. As the hot water ran down his back, he mused to himself: why another shower? He had done no physical work for the day; he wasn't dirty or sweaty. He even splashed some aftershave on his face, a rare event. He put on a clean pair of trousers and a clean shirt. He would have to do some ironing one of these days but it was a job he hated and wasn't very good at. By seven-thirty he had crossed the driveway and was ringing Alison's bell.

Unfortunately, she wasn't wearing the tight jeans this evening, a baggy fawn trouser suit instead. At least he thought it was fawn. He wasn't very good at colours beyond the primary ones. He guessed that somewhere in junior high school he must have been absent the day the art teacher articulated the names of all the colours. Katriona was much better with colours. He would say that something was blue. She would retort that it was navy. He would say, 'Aren't blue and navy the same?' 'They're completely different,' she would say. Anyway, she would be able to describe the colour of Alison's trouser suit now, had she been there. Lane kissed her on the cheek and presented her with the flowers and the wine.

Her perfume hit his nostrils like an aromatic shock wave. It dawned on him that he had not had a whiff of perfume for weeks. It was strange how something so familiar could go missing without you becoming aware of it.

Alison ushered him into the lounge and invited him to sit. She disappeared to find a vase for the flowers. The lounge was a nice square shape, and his corner chair was comfortable. It was good to sit back in someone else's easy chair and have them cater for you for a little while. Alison and Neil had good taste, and Neil had been a competent DIY man. He had framed most of the pictures on the walls in the lounge, including a Vettriano print—the *Singing Butler*—popular with most everyone in the world except the critics. Lane had been in so many houses where there was virtually nothing on the walls. He couldn't understand how people could live without art or decoration of some kind. One of his lecturers in seminary had said that the walls of a room always teach, and that was true. Did empty walls signify an empty life? Even a ceramic flight of ascending ducks was better than nothing. Through the archway he watched Alison light the candles on the table. Beyond the table, patio doors looked out on the back garden, adjacent to his own. But Alison's garden was very colorful, neat and tidy, and it made him feel guilty.

Alison returned and stood, looking down at him, hands on her hips. 'Now, Davis,' she asked, 'what can I get you to drink—a whisky? I don't think I have any—what is it you like again?'

'Lagavulin,' said Lane.

'I don't have any Lagavulin, but what about Glenfiddich?' she asked.

'That's fine,' Lane replied. 'I like Glenfiddich.'

'It's what Neil usually drank,' Alison said. 'Neat or with water?'

'Just some water,' Lane answered.

Alison returned with the drinks and sat down on the couch opposite Lane. She was, he thought once again, a nice looking woman. She was slim, had good colour, and her hair was redder than he had remembered. She possessed a kind of cheerfulness that he liked.

'So what are you doing to keep busy these days?' Alison asked.

'I've got a project on,' said Lane. 'There is a company in Edinburgh that has asked me to do some research and writing for them.'

'What company is that?' she asked.

Lane had been afraid this question would be put. It might prove difficult to explain convincingly. 'The Clan Caledonia Company,' he answered. 'They export a lot of Scottish things to America: kilts and rugs and maps of the distilleries and so forth. They need some material for their products and their advertising blurbs. So that's what I'm doing.' He would try to keep it as vague as possible.

'I didn't know that you did advertising,' Alison said, a faint smile on her face. 'Do you mean that highland dress has theological implications?'

She was smart, thought Lane; he would need to construct a more convincing scenario. 'Well, you know how seriously these people in the States take their Scottish lineage,' he offered. 'They get deeply involved, finding out about their ancestry on the net, then coming over to trace the family through church records and in the registry office. Some of them now want to go back even further into the past. They want to know all about the Celts and about St. Columba landing on Iona and so on. Anything that has to do with early Scottish history or the clans seems to be appealing. So I'm looking into that with a view towards writing little historical summaries that could be included when their orders are shipped.'

'I see,' said Alison, nodding understandingly. 'That could be interesting, then?'

'It is actually,' answered Lane, feeling very guilty now about this line. 'Being educated in the United States, I never really got much in the way of Scottish history, so this is completing my education in a way.' He hoped that this would terminate this particular conversation.

Alison saved him. 'Give me a minute,' she said. 'I think that the dinner is about ready. Would you mind opening the wine? Neil always did that.'

'I'll be glad to,' said Lane, relieved to be let off the hook for a while.

They sat down at the table and he was asked to say the grace. During the starter and the main course they chatted about what Alison had been doing: her golf, her peeves about the local church and her problems with her elderly mother. Lane told her everything he knew about Katriona's work.

After Alison had served desert, Lane a question to her: 'Alison, how are you, really, I mean?'

She was reflective for a moment, looking down and toying with the stem of her wine glass. She looked up at Lane and was surprisingly deliberate in her response. 'I'm not so bad, I suppose, but I could be better. I just miss Neil so much. I come home and there is no one there, no one is expected, and no one ever comes in. You have news from the day you want to share—just simple things—and there is no one to share it with. I go round the garden and want to point out things to him, and he isn't there. I wake up in the morning, and he isn't there. I have a little bubble now and then and I suppose it helps. But it just seems all so empty and pointless somehow.'

'Yes, it must do,' said Lane. 'What's the worse time for you, at night or in the morning?'

Alison thought for a moment. 'Probably at night. I just lie awake and think about it. I go over everything that happened again and again.'

'Are you angry?' Lane asked.

'Am I angry?' She looked out into the distance through the patio window, contemplating the question. 'Well, yes, I suppose I am.'

'I mean, angry at God?' asked Lane.

'Not so much angry as confused…but yes, I suppose I am angry as well. But that's wrong, isn't it?' she answered. 'You're not supposed to be angry with God. It's like saying that you don't have faith in him.'

'That's what most people think,' Lane suggested. 'But that's really to misunderstand things. If you look in the Bible you'll find that lots of the characters there get angry with God for what happens to them. They blame him, shout at him, and even curse him at times, and yet they are regarded as saints. Look, did you and Neil ever disagree about anything?'

'Of course,' said Alison. 'Like everyone else, we had our ups and downs.'

'OK,' said Lane. 'Did you ever get angry at him and shout at him?'

'Sure,' said Alison. 'He shouted at me sometimes, too.' She was clasping her hands in her lap and her eyes were watery. Lane softened his tone.

'Exactly,' he said, 'you had a deep relationship with each other. You had a conversation that lasted a long time, and in that kind of conversation you do get angry and blame and shout at each other. Faith doesn't mean the absence of doubt; it means having confidence in being able to express it. Faith in God is really the willingness to have a conversation that lasts a lifetime. So it is okay to get angry and blame God for what happens to you. He understands that, even if he isn't responsible for everything that happens to us. A lot of life is determined by chance.'

'I suppose so,' she said, 'but does it ever get any better? My friends keep saying that time will heal the wound, but so far that hasn't happened.'

'Yes, I wish that people would stop saying that,' Lane said. 'It's one of these clichés that keep getting repeated regardless of the facts. Time doesn't do anything except pass and mark the duration of our grief. Things will get better, but that sense of loss will always be there. The wound heals over, but you'll always be able to feel the scar. It's a physical thing as well as being mental and emotional. It's like losing a part of your own body. People don't know that going through grief is like having an amputation. I visited a member of mine in hospital once. As we talked, he kept looking down as his right foot. I finally asked him about it.

He looked up at me and said, 'They're taking it off tomorrow.' That was all he said: 'They're taking it off tomorrow.' It must have been terrible, studying one of your limbs and knowing that it wouldn't be there the next day. And losing your partner is like losing a very large part of your own being.'

Alison nodded but said nothing. She had slipped down in her chair and seemed diminished. She also looked close to tears. How devastated by loss we really are, he thought. He hadn't really intended to slip into the pastoral role that evening, but it was surprising sometimes how it inserted itself into relationships, even when you weren't trying. He had probably gone on too long about grief. Time to shut up and go home. If he had showered and put on aftershave for any semi-conscious ulterior motive…, well forget it. She needed to have the comfort of arms wrapped around her, which he could do; that much was allowed. But in her vulnerable state he would not take advantage of her.

They moved back to the lounge for coffee. Alison asked about whether he had plans to visit Katriona. Lane tried to explain that things were uncertain about how long this project and the income from it would last. They talked about the gardens and the weather, and the peculiar social system of Inverkeithing. At eleven Lane suggested that he ought to be going. He thanked her for the evening.

'Davis,' she said, 'I'm sorry for getting upset, but it has been good. I've really enjoyed talking tonight. You've helped me a lot. Thank you for coming.'

Alison,' he offered, 'thank you for inviting me. I've enjoyed it. Would you let me make a meal for you sometime? I'm not too bad a cook, you know.'

'I'm sure that you're a good cook,' she said, 'but are you sure? You're going to be very busy.'

'Of course, I'm sure. I'll be in touch and we'll arrange a date.'

He put his arms around her, hugged her for a moment, and went to kiss her cheek. But she didn't turn her face and he made an awkward encounter with both her lips and her cheek. When he tried to extract himself, she seemed reluctant to let him go.

Back in the bathroom of his own house, Lane studied himself in the mirror while he brushed his teeth. Who was he and what was he doing? Relationships were confusing; you got so many conflicting signals. He thought he had done a fair job as a friend/pastor that evening, but had more been required? What had Alison expected of the evening? What had he expected? He believed absolutely that we needed to be channels of God's grace for each other, but the channels were never pre-formed. What happened when the channel of grace might cut across the rules and customs of your society? What happened when they might cut across your own rules and principles? How far were you to go to love your neighbor? The church had never handled the theology of sex well, and now it was hopelessly exploited by the society. Lane studied his puzzling reflection in the mirror for moment and then headed for bed.

CHAPTER 9

▼

When Lane went online the next morning he had several new emails. One was especially welcome. He read as follows:

Dear Davis

Sorry it has taken so long to respond to your last email. It has been so busy at work. We went to Antigua the other day to see what the workers are doing there, and it was very interesting. But it was after 11 before we got back and I was exhausted.

I don't know how I can ever adjust to life back in the UK. The affluence that we enjoy seems just obscene here in Guatemala City. My work is getting focussed on the kids who live in the centre of the city. Most are orphans or street kids. They have nothing and spend most of their time hanging around some of the better apartment buildings dumpster diving. While one of them keeps an eye open for the police, the others haul themselves into the large bins used for rubbish collection. They literally go through everything looking for money or shoes or anything that could be sold. They get to be really adept at it, but the poverty they live in is unbelievable. We try to get them involved in a programme of some kind, but they are very wary. I sometimes dream about them at night.

Your new job sounds great, and it will be good to have an income, but I don't see what the connection is between Clan Caledonia and theology. You'll need to tell me more. Must go now and get some sleep.

Love

K. XXX

Lane was glad to hear from his wife, but the truth was he felt a little depressed after reading her email. It was hard to put his finger on it. It was the bit about adjusting to life once she returned to the UK. He understood perfectly well the gap between the affluence between here and the poverty in so many other places in the world. They had seen it before every time they visited the States: big cars, big houses, wasted food, excessive consumption all round. He shared her abhorrence of that gap, but at the same time, they were just making good their big transition from the parish and manse to their own style of life. He didn't want to embrace wholeheartedly the affluence of the west, but he also didn't know if he could face another period of upset and uncertainty. Please Katriona, he thought, let's just give ourselves time to arrive at a stable state.

Back to the book. Lane was now up to May 4 in *My Utmost for His Highest*, but it was proving slower going than he had anticipated. This was not because the writing was theologically heavy, but because it didn't seem to go anywhere. It was a theological *cul de sac*. The way that Chambers started from a text but then engaged in nomadic interpretive wandering meant that there was little consistency. Chambers' "disciplined" thought for the day never appeared to lead to much concrete advice about living in a complex world. Rather, it almost always led merely to the counsel to abandon yourself to God, to identify with God, to surrender to God, and more of the same. The real world dissolved in the ascetic acid of intimacy with His Highest. Chambers' theology implied a cosmological bypass. So much for God's good creation.

Concentrating hard on a page, Lane jumped when the telephone rang.

'Hello Davis, this is Robert McCord. How are you doing?'

'Hello,' replied Lane, 'I'm fine, but this book is really hard going. You caught me toiling in the middle of a passage which makes no sense.'

'Glad to hear that you're working. I'm on my mobile,' said McCord, 'so I don't want to talk for long. Could we meet for lunch tomorrow and you can tell me what you think so far? I know it's too early for a detailed report, but I'd just like to know where you think it's heading.'

'Yes, sure,' said Lane. 'Where do you want to meet?'

'Somewhere different,' McCord replied. 'I'll head out your direction and save you the trouble of coming all the way into the city. Is there somewhere local where we can eat and talk in private?'

'What about Dalgety Bay?' Lane answered. 'There's a pub called the Hope Tryst. It's a little run down, but the food is good and it's cheap. It's in the centre of the Bay, the Regent's Way.'

'Fine,' said McCord. 'But you'd better tell me how to get to Dalgety Bay. I haven't a clue'

It was typical, thought Lane. People had heard of the Bay but had no idea where it actually was. The town was like Garrison Keillor's Lake Wobegon, always lying in the fold of the map. Their friends from Edinburgh had at first visualized it as a long way away. In the early days after they moved, their dinner guests habitually arrived far too early, under the impression that it would take hours to get there. He gave directions to McCord.

'Fine,' McCord said. 'I'll see you about one.'

Lane was about to agree, but McCord had abruptly hung up. The line was dead. The man certainly didn't waste any time on the phone. This hastily arranged meeting the next day brought him up short. To produce some hard copy he would need to apply himself even more diligently.

Lane worked solidly on the book for the next few hours. Finally, he felt ready to write a little summary of what he had found so far. He wrote as follows:

Some Preliminary Notes:
My Utmost for His Highest: January 1-May 5

Oswald Chambers does not appear to fit neatly into any theological niche. As you probably know, the Protestant Reformation of the sixteenth century brought into being three distinct groups: the Lutherans, the Calvinists, and the Anabaptists. In the last four centuries a bewildering number of churches, groups, and movements have arisen to shape the history of Christianity. Chambers would probably best be called a "Pietist", with his emphasis on conversion, regeneration, the importance of feeling, the life of piety, and an ascetic approach to the world. He also shares some attitudes of those who were part of the Great Awakening in Britain and America, but differs from them by an apparent lack of interest in church structures and in charitable work in the world.

In this book Oswald Chambers provides a devotional reflection for each day of the year, one day per page. A title and a text from the Old or New Testaments is provided in each case. Chambers' interpretation of scripture is highly selective in that he does not explore the context of the text or go into the passage quoted in any significant detail. There is no evidence that he has read the passage in the original language (Hebrew and Greek) or consulted any of the biblical scholars in order to better inform himself. Chambers is prone to bring in several altogether different passages in the course of a single devotion in order to support his thesis. The passage is therefore used mainly as a springboard for his own preferred message, which many would find to be at considerable variance from the commonly understood meaning of the passage itself.

Chambers' theology appears to be roughly as follows: When the Holy Spirit comes to a person he *invades* (Chambers' own terms) the person, changing him and setting him onto a new course of ever increasing intimacy with God. Terms used in this process of dying and having a new life include that of having a *white funeral* (a new one to me) and *sanctification*. In the process of sanctification, the believer is born again from above, which is an enduring, perpetual and eternal beginning. Chambers speaks of those habits and of an unholy nature that must die. During this process the true believer becomes much closer to God, so that other people pale in comparison with God himself. The believer's personal holiness increases as he becomes more and more intimate with God, leading to purification, separation and the elimination of desire, affection and dejection. Complete surrender to God leads to the personal holiness that draws others to God, rather than to any specific activity or intercession for them. What matters is not a sympathetic understanding of others, but one's own identification with God on their behalf. It may be, Chambers argues, that God is causing their darkness in order to lead them to himself. The activities of Christian workers are often criticized, for they are based on busyness or on the believer's own ideas rather than on what God reveals to his intimates. Faith means faith alone, and so understanding and reason are devalued. Believers must seek to grow in *purity*; it is in contact with other people and other points of view that we become *tarnished*. The true believer should never allow questions that are unsound or unbalanced to disturb him and should never display any doubts that come to him.

When it comes to the moral behaviour of the believer in the world, intimacy with God means that moral behaviour is automatic. The characteristic of love is spontaneity, implying that a thoughtful course of moral action is not required. Identification with God yields a complete obedience, and obedience automatically yields the right moral action. He cites Abraham, for example, who was ready to do anything for God. One particular devotion, that for March 20 is crucial in this respect. It provides an accurate summary, and I quote it here.

This friendship means being so intimately in touch with God that you never even need to ask Him to show you His will. It is evidence of a level of intimacy which confirms that you are nearing the final stage of your discipline in the life of faith. When you have a right-standing relationship with God, you have a life of freedom, liberty and delight; you are God's will. And all of your commonsense decisions are actually His will for you, unless you sense a feeling of restraint brought on by a check of your spirit.

Analysis: On the whole, Chambers' devotional theology is broadly in line with what has historically been called the Pietist tradition. However, the liberty he takes in his interpretation of scripture probably represents a departure even from that tradition. His emphasis on "feeling" does convey some of the warmth of the Pietists, but that warmth is dissipated by attitude towards those who remain unconverted. His theology as a whole is in very wide variance with the theology of the Reformed tradition of the church. In most Christian theology, the person of faith remains a sinner, even if he makes progress in growing in faith. So "sanctification" is real in the sense that virtues such as love grow, but it is never held that a person becomes so intimate with God that he is the will of God. St Paul is very clear about the persistence of sin. The entire discipline of Christian Ethics exists because doing what is "good" or "right" is not easy. The idea that good or right could flow automatically from the sanctified person is highly suspect.

With reference to the reading of this material by the person in question, I would say that it poses certain very real dangers. If a person with real and substantial powers of state were to take seriously the idea that his decisions and actions were identical with the will of God, then the results could prove to be disastrous. This, however, is only a preliminary judgement for there is much more of the book to study and analyse.

Prepared by Davis Lane, Freelance Theologian

Lane saved what he had written and closed down. He hoped that this was the sort of thing that McCord wanted. It was quite difficult to try to write theologically when the society was theologically ignorant. It no longer possessed even the basic vocabulary to think or converse about these matters. But it had been a long day and he was tired. He hadn't even had time to reply to Katriona. It was tough when you couldn't even be bothered to put on a CD and have a dram.

CHAPTER 10

▼

When Lane drew back his curtains the next morning, it looked like a thick grey blanket had been pulled up over the Firth of Forth. The world had become opaque overnight. The bridges could not be seen, nor could Hound Point. A fog-horn had been sounding periodically throughout the night and was still intimating danger, attributing an eerie quality to the world. Lane studied the scene from his window. The fog always made the ordinary mysterious: you knew that there was maritime traffic in the Firth: tankers, freighters, and the ferry, all on their way up or down the water, but you could see nothing. They were all moving stealthily under the blanket. Thank God for radar, he thought.

He had a quick breakfast and wandered a little reluctantly into the study. For the next two hours he worked on his preliminary report for McCord, checking his interpretation yet again and refining his analysis. He printed off the report and placed it into an envelope, hoping it would do as a start.

The Hope Tryst was situated in the Regent's Way or Metro Centre of Dalgety Bay. Lane always thought that the name "Metro" gave a false impression. When you saw "Metro", you thought about the urban traffic area of cities like New York or Paris. You thought subway trains and buses and shops and streets jammed with commuters. But the Metro Centre Way of Dalgety Bay couldn't have been much more than one hundred metres square. It was only a square parking lot enclosed on two sides by shops. True, there were lots of parked cars, but no trains or buses, apart from an occasional visit from Melvin's Mobile Barber Shop.

The Bay was really a New Town, one of the first in Scotland, but unlike the other New Towns it had been privately developed. There had been a much older community here known as Dalgety Parish. Lane had read that the residents, called Dalgeties, had come originally from Denmark to escape religious persecution. Whole families had been involved in mining the high-grade coal of the area. Their foreignness and harsh living conditions had prescribed an inclusive community, in which intermarriage and inbreeding had produced a somewhat odd community. But the Dalgeties were now long lost in the past. These days the Bay was basically a bedroom community of better quality housing with well-kept gardens set on wide streets. It kept winning the prize for Best Kept Small Town in West Fife, but that didn't make it cosmopolitan. Nothing much ever happened in the Bay. Lane had once seen a newspaper hoarding with the main headline announcing "New Bio-Bins for the Bay". That was about as exciting as it got.

The post office, supermarket, newspaper and video shops, and several other small businesses lay on one side of the square. On the other side was the travel agent, bank, estate agent, chemist and finally the pub. The Hope Tryst had seen better days. Its paint was cracked and peeling, and the picnic tables in the garden rotten and ragged. Still, the place was friendly, and the food was cheap and remarkably good. He assumed that Francis, the lady behind the bar, was the owner/manager. She seemed solely in charge. He'd only caught glimpses of someone else, presumably the cook, through the kitchen door. Francis was efficient, pulling pints, taking orders, serving food and clearing tables at an astonishing rate.

Lane surveyed the Tryst as he drove into the parking lot. The idea that he was about to rendezvous with an agent of the CIA in this setting seemed absolutely ludicrous. He reversed the Cruiser into a parking place next to the recycling bins and waited. Ten minutes later he watched as McCord drove in and parked his silver Saab. Emerging from the car he looked slightly bewildered. Lane walked over and greeted him.

'Is this it?' asked McCord. 'Is this all there is?'

'I'm afraid so,' said Lane. 'Were you expecting more?'

'I didn't know what to expect,' said McCord. 'When I asked my secretary and several friends in Edinburgh about Dalgety Bay, they couldn't tell me much. They said it was somewhere in Fife, but they didn't know where. It seems like a mystery town.'

Lane laughed. 'It's hardly a town, more like a village. But that's typical. It's kind of a well-kept secret. I sometimes think of it as a mythological place, People across the water have heard of it but don't know anything about it or where it is or how to get to it. But you know it isn't a myth when you get your council tax bill'

They were walking towards the Tryst when McCord pointed to the large banner stretched along the fence at the back of the place. '"All meals £2.99." That can't be right?'

'It is,' said Lane. 'All the meals are £2.99, and they're OK.'

The Tryst was better heeled inside than it was outside. The windows of the restaurant were on the west side, and the tables in that section were bathed in light. Preferring the light, Lane normally sat there, even though it was the smoking area. The non-smoking area on the other side of the room was far enough away from the windows to be very dark. A single wall fixture shed a little light on the tables. Lane led McCord to the bar and handed him a menu. 'What would you like to drink?'

'Whatever you're having,' said McCord. While Francis was pulling their pints, Lane selected some cutlery and pointed McCord to the condiments. 'You'll be glad to know that the tomato sauce is in packets here, and you can take as many as you can carry,' he said.

Without a trace of a smile, McCord replied, 'Great' and lifted half-a-dozen packets from the container. The two men collected their pints from the bar and headed for a table. Lane started to move in the direction of the windows, but McCord headed straight and without hesitation to the other, darker side of the room. They found a table and sat down. McCord took a seat against the wall, and for a long moment studied the door and the other customers. Finally, he turned back to look at Lane and raised his glass.

'Cheers. How are you getting on, then?'

'Cheers,' Lane answered. 'Not too bad. I'm up to the month of May in the book. It's tedious stuff, but the analysis part is getting more interesting as I go along. I've made some preliminary notes for you.' Lane reached into his jacket pocket and extracted the white envelope. He held on to it, while Francis arrived bringing napkins and salt and pepper. When she departed, Lane handed the envelope to McCord, who still seemed distracted.

'Do you mind if I open this now?' asked McCord. 'I'd like to take a quick look.'

'Sure,' said Lane, taking another drink of the Belhaven.

McCord opened the flap of the envelope. He seemed almost painstakingly careful as he pulled out the two pages that Lane had prepared. For a tall man, he had delicate hands and used them gracefully. Francis came with their plates and set them on the table. McCord scarcely noticed. He read intently while Lane ate his scampi. McCord finished the second page and then went back to the first page and started again. Lane was almost done eating when McCord finally folded the paper, replaced it in the envelope and placed it into his jacket pocket.

'Is that the sort of thing you're looking for?' asked Lane.

'It's great, perfect,' replied McCord, beginning to attack his food now.

Lane waited while the other man ate. When McCord stopped to take a drink, Lane said, 'There's still quite a bit to analyze in the book. I just wanted to make sure that I was producing what you are looking for.'

'You're on the right track,' McCord said. 'But don't worry too much about setting Chambers in some theological context. I have no idea what you mean when you say that he is a Pietist. We're not interested in that as much as in the implications of what he says. Now I'm anxious to see what you find in the rest of the book. What do you think of what you've read so far? Do you think we ought to have serious concerns about the particular dedicated reader we have in mind?'

'It depends,' said Lane. 'I think it depends on how seriously the person you have in mind takes all this stuff. If it's just a little waking-up-in-the-morning exercise, a reminder of where he's come from and what he needs to avoid, then no problem. But if he really does take it seriously—at least Chambers' idea of the final stage of intimacy with God—then I would be pretty worried.'

McCord laid down his cutlery, dabbed his mouth with his napkin and leaned forward on the table as he had done in the office of Clan Caledonia. Lane leaned forward in response. McCord spoke now in a low voice. 'In your opinion, Davis, would the person we are talking about be vulnerable to outside influence or even manipulation if he took *My Utmost* seriously?'

Lane considered this for a moment and then replied. 'I would have to say yes.'

McCord leaned back in his seat and grimaced. 'I thought you might say that,' he offered.

'But,' said Lane, 'the danger wouldn't arise simply from outside influence. Were your man to take Chambers really seriously and act on his own bat it could be a disaster.'

McCord studied Lane and nodded but said nothing. Silence enveloped them. Lane had intended at this meeting to get to know McCord better, to ask about his personal life. Where was he from? Was he married, and if so, did he have children? But now, in this oppressive silence, all that went by the board.

The two men finished their beer in silence, got up from the table and headed towards the door. Lane waved to Francis on the way out. Outside, on the way to the car park, McCord stopped and took Lane's arm. 'Now,' he said, 'There is something you need to understand. We know that the other parties I spoke to you about are scouting around to see what they can find. Have you told anybody about what you're doing?'

'Only two people,' said Lane. 'I sent an email to Katriona my wife, and I told my neighbour that I had a project to do for Clan Caledonia.'

'OK,' McCord said. 'You can simply go on with the line that you're doing work for Clan Caledonia, but don't be more specific than that. I don't want you to mention what you are doing in any more emails. The Internet is not secure. And don't talk about it on the phone. That's even less secure. Whatever you do, don't use the phone to contact Clan Caledonia. I'll get in touch with you. If you do have to ring me in an emergency, use your mobile and phone me on my mobile. Even then keep it short.' McCord handed him a card with a mobile number written on it. No name, just a number.

Halfway into the car park now, Lane felt suddenly short of breath and paused.

'What are you saying?' asked Lane. 'Do you really mean that there is some kind of danger?'

'Not danger exactly,' said McCord. 'It's just that these other people would really like to get their hands on this information, and we would rather they didn't.'

'When you say "we",' replied Lane, 'what do you mean?'

McCord put on an enigmatic smile. 'I mean Clan Caledonia, the Company,' he said, stretching out his right hand to Lane and using the remote in his left to unlock the car door. The two men shook hands and McCord got into his car. Lane walked to the Cruiser and realised that Melvin's bus was parked nearby. Melvin looked up from the head he was dealing with and gave Lane a wave. Lane waved back, but it was a half-hearted gesture.

Lane drove home slowly, still trying to get his head around what McCord had said. At Inverkeithing the fog had finally lifted and the sun was shining. The Bridges could be seen, and a tanker was being put into position at Hound Point. But Lane was preoccupied. He went inside and poured himself a dram. It was too early for a drink, but he needed one and he needed desperately to think things through. He put on a CD: Rhonda Vincent singing *One Step Ahead*:

> *Don't tell me that I'll be all right,*
> *That's somethin' you don't know.*
> *Don't tell me not to be uptight....*

CHAPTER 11

▼

The next morning Lane was up early, but not by choice. He had slept very badly, tossing and turning most of the night and constantly going over in his mind the conversation with Robert McCord. Yesterday had been bad. He had been severely limited, constrained by the very task that was supposed to offer some freedom: he was not to tell anyone what he was really up to; he was not to use the phone or email for significant communication because they were no longer secure; he was not even to try to contact the person for whom he was working. This work he had taken on was becoming absurd. Worse yet, McCord had said very clearly that other unspecified parties were interested in what he was doing. Did their *interest* mean that this was becoming dangerous? He was only doing a theological critique, for heaven's sake; why should he have to live with some unnamed menace? Was it really worth all this?

He had sat in front of the computer all morning with book in hand, trying to get into things, but the necessary focus wouldn't come. He had frittered away the afternoon, wandering around the house from one room to another, thinking about housework but doing nothing. He would have to do something else for a while, get away from the book and this train of thought. Surely he could take a day off in order to clear the mind. If he could get someone to go with him the next day, he would try a little fishing. He phoned Alex.

Alex Newbold had been Lane's senior elder in his church. Even in spite of that, they had become good friends. Alex had been a compositor at the *Scotsman*, but had retired when the technology altered nearly everything about the production of the paper. He had worked on for a while trying to use the new set-up, but it didn't really suit him. Early retirement was offered, so he took it. He would far rather be out on the golf course or on the loch. Lane was in luck. Alex had no plans for the next day and would be delighted to go.

They planned to meet at Loch Glow, a few miles northwest of Inverkeithing on the single-track road to Cleish. The early morning fog and the forest conspired to produce a surreal landscape. Fog drifted in and out of the branches of the standing pine and spruce. It hovered over the piles of brush where the forest had been cut, producing a scene of scarred desolation. Lane imagined that this could well have been some former battle zone in Eastern Europe. Even over the sound of the car engine the silence of the place seemed to take on weight and substance. It was definitely a little creepy, not exactly the sort of experience he had counted on. Suddenly, the waters of Loch Glow appeared through the trees and fog. Lane was surprised that even on a morning like this there were a number of cars in the parking lot, including Alex's. They greeted each other warmly and began to get their equipment ready.

The fishing club, who regularly stocked the loch, managed its daily use: collecting fees from anglers, keeping track of the catches, and maintaining the limited facilities. Volunteers from the club also manned the office, which took the form of an ancient caravan. This morning it was occupied by someone Lane had never seen before—a burly man in a tee shirt with tattoos on both arms. A large crow, obviously a pet, perched over him on the caravan roof as he leaned out of the window to take their money. As Lane held out his hand to collect their tickets, the crow flapped its wings and called loudly, as if accusing him of some trespass. He guessed they were invading the bird's territory. Lane thought about pinching himself to ascertain if this were real or a continuation of his dreams from the last night. The tattooed crow-master handed him two tickets for fishing and one for the use of a boat. The loch was good-sized, so that using a boat was a necessity if you were going to do serious fly-fishing. Most people remained on shore and were spinning with bait. Green and blue tents providing shelter from the wind already dotted the bank at regular intervals. The amount of equipment that people brought with them these days was staggering. The two men loaded their equipment into the boat. Alex would row out and Lane back.

The wind was from the west today, so Alex headed for that side, the shallower side of the loch. Once there they would begin casting, allowing the boat to drift east with the wind. Lane reckoned he would feel a bit happier when they were in position and had begun fishing in earnest. It took a lot of practice to get back into the rhythm of casting, especially when you hadn't been fishing for a while. This required concentration took your mind off other things. It was even better when you were river fishing. Through the current of the river and the pressure of the water against your hip waders, the water magically absorbed your anxieties. They floated downstream and far away.

They were near the far side of the loch now. Alex stopped rowing and quietly laid up the oars. The two men began to ready their lines. A large bird flew out of the timber on the north shore, hovered for a moment and then swooped down to lift a trout from the water. It was all so easy, so graceful. Lane suddenly decided that this must be an osprey. He had never imagined that there were ospreys so close to home. He wondered if it were true that the bird turned his catch in mid-air to make its flight more aerodynamic. In any event, it was a magnificent sight.

'So what have you been up to these days?' Alex asked, carefully inspecting his cast and letting out some line.

'I've got a couple of projects going,' Lane replied, 'mainly leading study groups in congregations and doing some research and writing.' He would need to watch himself here. 'What about you?'

'Oh, just dodging here and there you know.' Alex answered. 'Between the golf course and the church, I don't seem to have any time at all. I'm trying to get your successor trained, you know.' Alex turned his head and gave Lane a smile and a wink. Lane would have to monitor this topic of conversation as well. He didn't want to hear either negative or positive comments about the minister who had succeeded him in the parish. He believed that once you have left a place you should really leave it. He had heard of too many ministers who kept butting back into their old parishes, doing funerals and weddings. Of course, it was unrealistic to expect someone who had given a large part of his or her life over many years simply to disappear. It was about the only job he could think of where you were required to give up your work, your friends, and your house in one go, but still feel good about it. You might as well shoot the guy, to an accompanying chorus of 'Farewell, good and faithful servant.' You could hardly blame someone for wanting to have some contact with his or her old congregation now and then. But not him; he had hung up his Bible and ridden off into the west, having done what he felt was a creditable job. He wanted to stay lost in the west.

'Is it time for lunch yet, Alex?' Lane asked, grinning. This was a standing joke between them. Whenever they went fishing, Alex was always keen to have his lunch almost immediately after they arrived. He loved a turkey sandwich, a packet of crisps and a can of beer, followed by an apple. Alex turned towards Lane with a hurt expression on his face. 'Come on, now, Davis' he said.

Lane tried his first cast, and it was pathetic. It would take him a while to get back into the action. He envied Alex, whose line was shooting out effortlessly and taking his flies far downwind.

'How do you like being retired Alex?' Lane asked. 'Are you missing your old job these days?'

Alex had been retrieving the leader slowly, but now stopped and turned to look at Lane. 'Not really, Davis. It's a different world now. The job I did doesn't exist anymore. It's all done electronically. To be honest with you, I rarely buy the newspapers these days. It's not just the technology; it's the content. I can hardly bear reading the papers. It's all flash with little substance. You can tell that from the headlines. They are designed to convey sensation, but they don't bear any relation to the story. No, it's too superficial.' Alex shook his head as if he needed to dismiss the whole idea.

Yes, I know what you mean and I tend to agree,' Lane said, 'but I guess that's what sells newspapers: sensation and sex. Sex sells everything these days.' It was another hobbyhorse of his, but he didn't feel like pursuing it at the moment. He was here to unwind, after all. Anyway, trying to recover his ability to use the fly rod was sufficient challenge.

They fished in silence for a while. The boat was drifting faster now as the wind was up. Lane had made another bad cast. He was sitting trying to untangle the flies. He should have remembered to put a pin in his lapel for that job.

Alex finally broke the silence: 'The other thing that gets me about the papers,' he said, 'is the constant focus on celebrities. We are constantly being told who the celebs are going out with, who they are divorcing, what they are wearing and what their fortune is worth.' He made a bad cast, shook his head and brought in line immediately. 'I don't want to know what these stars are doing. I haven't even heard of most of these people.'

'Maybe they're in a very distant galaxy,' Lane responded to mutual laughter, 'and the light hasn't reached us yet.'

Newbold chuckled while making another long, perfect cast. Absorbed in fishing now, he didn't turn around when he spoke. 'We may not be interested in the stars,' he said, 'but it seems like most people are. I was thinking the other day that I could never be a contestant on a TV quiz show because all the questions are about the stars of *Eastenders* or *Coronation Street*. Do you know, Davis, that I have never seen *Eastenders*?'

Lane laughed. 'No kidding! Join the club, Alex.' He had sorted out his line and made another cast that was okay but still short. 'I don't get all that worked up about the stars but I do about the media itself. It seems to me that actually the media have become the real power in the world today, at least in democratic countries. They control what people think and believe and do. It's all very subtle of course; we just take it for granted. It appears that they are simply providing information. But they shape our lives more than the government does. I mean, have you noticed how much of the news each day is about politics? The coverage is constant. They focus so hard on politics that the whole process becomes distorted. There is no longer any real room for just discussing issues and deciding on a course of action. Toss out an idea one day and the next the media is presenting it as hard policy and stirring up opposition. And no one is in a position to criticize all this. An academic might offer some critique of broadcasting, or you and I might do it. But it goes nowhere because the media own the only effective channels of communication. It's not so much that the media is the message or even the massage; it's the media is the master.' Lane was so involved in his own message that he had neglected to cast.

'Now Davis,' Newbold piped up, 'I seem to remember some sermons about that.'

'Yes, you're right, Alex. I'm sorry. I didn't mean to go on,' Davis said.

'We're here to fish,' Alex said. 'Anyway, I don't think it's quite that bad. We get a lot of important information these days, especially from the radio. And some of the entertainment programmes are very good.'

Lane didn't seem to take this on board. He was still sitting, reflecting over the water. 'The other thing that gets me, though,' he said, 'is how the media treat religion. We now have about two generations of people who have become detached from the church. They don't know what the faith or the church is about. When they come to weddings or baptisms, they haven't a clue about what to do or how to behave.' He stood up suddenly and made a cast, actually not a bad one. He reckoned it was an anger cast. 'It would be good if the media were interested enough to provide some accurate and deeper coverage of religion. I mean, shouldn't that be part of their job? But no, they would much rather find some kind of salacious gossip about the ministry or the church and push it to the hilt: "Minister runs off with lady organist"—that sort of thing.'

Alex had stopped casting and was letting his flies sink in the water, watching and listening intently. He'd never seen his ex-minister become so animated. 'I know what you mean,' he said, 'but you've got to remember that editors don't think of religious news as very important. They channel most of it to young reporters. They've never been connected to the church, so they don't know anything. How can you blame them?'

'Of course,' Lane said. 'But what happens is that they deepen the existing ignorance by writing stuff that bears no relation to what is the case. They really know very little about the Christian faith, and even less about the church. So instead of enlightening the world they are making it darker.' He stopped again to make another cast.

'They don't even have the basic vocabulary,' Lane said. 'They aren't knowledgeable enough to write about faith or hope or love. They could never handle ideas like confession or repentance or sanctification.' Hearing himself speak these words suddenly turned his mind back to Oswald Chambers' idea of sanctification. But with some effort he pushed this to the back of his mind and went on. 'They keep talking about ministers who lose their faith. God, as if faith were a £5 note that you could lose somewhere. Hey, you haven't seen my faith anywhere, have you? I'm sure I had it in my wallet earlier, but I can't find it now.'

'Now, Davis,' Alex said, trying to move into a new mode, 'you asked me about my retirement, but how about yours? Are you enjoying life? Are you missing the congregation?'

'Of course I am,' Lane answered. 'I miss the people and I miss the discipline of trying to say something relevant every week. I guess that's why I've been going on this morning.' Lane suddenly felt a jerk on the line. He set the hook and began to play a fish. After a minute, Newbold moved over with the net and lifted the fish from the water. It was a fourteen-inch rainbow. 'Hey,' said Alex, 'I've heard of anger golf but never anger fishing! Well done.'

'I'll throw this one back, will I?' Lane asked.

'No, no,' Newbold answered. 'You don't throw fish back anymore. You practice "hug and release."'

'What?' Lane asked, thinking that his hearing had suddenly deteriorated.

'Hug and release,' Newbold responded. 'I saw it the other day on a website about fishing in Canada. You hug the fish and then release it.'

'Okay,' Lane answered. 'I'll release it, but it's too small and wet to hug.'

Three hours, one lunch, and three released fish later they made their way back to shore. They wrote up the catch in the returns box, packed up their equipment, and waved to the tattooed man and his crow. Neither made any response. They shook hands and promised to be in contact soon to arrange another fishing trip.

On the way home, Lane decided that he was feeling better. It was surprising how even a little diversion could lift you. Catching a couple of trout could help you forget your anxieties and give you confidence once again. It was ridiculous really, but that's what life was like. What he also knew but failed to recall was how quickly life could bring you down again.

CHAPTER 12

▼

Once he was on the road and headed home, Lane put Johnny Cash in the player and began to think himself back into the project. He was feeling better about things now; a day's fishing could work wonders. He felt a surge of confidence about being able to deal with the limitations that McCord had imposed. The fact that other unknown parties were *interested* shouldn't bother him so much. Let them be interested; it was no skin off his back. Just get on with the work.

By the time he pulled into the driveway he was feeling good. The sun was shining down and things were looking up. Alison was working in her front garden. She was on her knees beside a large blue container overflowing with weeds. She looked up and gave him a wave. As he got out of the car and walked towards the house, she called to him. As Lane reached the edge of her driveway, she pushed a handful of weeds into the tub, blew the hair away from her eyes, and stood up.

'Alison,' he said, 'I'm sorry that I haven't got back to you yet about coming over for dinner, but…'

She interrupted him: 'Davis, that's OK; I didn't wave you over for that reason. Don't worry about it. But when did you change your window cleaner? Is there some problem with Billy? Is he unwell or something?'

'Sorry, Alison, I'm not with you. What do you mean?' he asked. Most of the houses in the neighborhood had their windows cleaned by Billy and his team. For all he knew, Billy serviced all of the windows in Inverkeithing. He'd never seen a competitor in the area. Billy and his father and brothers appeared regularly once a month with their ladders and squeegees and stealthily surrounded the house. It was like a covert operation. They did the job even if you weren't at home, depositing a card through the door to inform you that they had been and what you owed. Sometimes Lane reckoned that Billy's year actually possessed thirteen months, but it didn't matter; they were always fast, efficient and courteous. Billy was short and stocky, with broad shoulders and blonde hair. He was an easygoing, happy type of guy with plenty to say. He might well spend more time talking to you at the door than actually washing windows. Last year he got married and had stood on the doorstep telling Lane more than he really wanted to know about their honeymoon in Barbados. Lane guessed that window cleaning couldn't be too bad if you could afford to honeymoon in Barbados. Billy's team all dressed in the same kind of blue overalls. They never rang the bell to announce their presence before starting work; the intimation of their presence came when a pair of blue overalls appeared on a ladder at your window. It could give you a real fright. And if you weren't up yet or just coming out of the shower, well...

Alison went on: 'Well, I saw this man on his ladder at your window. He wasn't in blue so I knew he wasn't one of Billy's guys. Anyway, he was all by himself. He didn't come here asking to clean my windows, and I didn't see him at any other house, so I was just curious. Why did you change window cleaners?'

'I didn't,' said Lane, trying to work out what was going on here. 'I don't know who that could have been. I'm very happy with Billy. I'm at a loss, Alison. I don't know who that was. I think I should go and check the house.'

'Of course,' said Alison, 'on you go. I'll see you later.'

Lane unlocked the door and went into the house. The place didn't look like it had been disturbed. The back door was still locked. The patio door was locked. The window in his bedroom was open, but he always opened it at night before he went to bed. He had a thing about needing fresh air to sleep. He usually shut it during the day. Had he closed the window this morning? He couldn't remember. The key had broken in the lock earlier that year, so it couldn't actually be locked.

He went into the study. It looked intact. The desk drawers and the file drawers were all shut. The computer was still there. He could see no sign that anyone had been in the study. Except...except that the blind on the window was down a little, only about a foot. The previous owners of the house had used this room as a bedroom for one of their boys, who had obviously been a Manchester United fan. The whole room was done in Manchester United wallpaper and colours, including the red blind on the window. Lane had repapered the room—one of his first DIY tasks. But he hadn't been able to remove the blind. It was very stiff, and he didn't want to force it down. So he had left that job for a later date. It was on his mental DIY list. But now the blind was down about a foot. It wasn't like that before, was it? He tried to remember.

He sat down at the computer workstation and studied it. Where was his floppy disk, the disk he used to write up his analysis of *My Utmost for His Highest*? His heart sank. It wasn't under the monitor, where he usually put it. It wasn't in the drive, and it wasn't in the little plastic file box where he kept his other disks. It was gone. His heart was pounding now, and he was beginning to feel sick in the pit of the stomach. He turned on the pc and waited. He put in the password and waited some more. After what seemed like an age, his icons appeared and he double clicked Word. He went into File and clicked Open. Sure enough, *My Utmost* was at the top of the list. Somebody had opened the file. Or had they? Wasn't that the last thing he had worked on? It would have been there anyway. How could you tell if it had been opened? He hadn't saved his work on the hard disk; whoever was here would have needed the floppy.

Lane sat still, staring at the screen, feeling stunned. He couldn't believe that someone had violated their house and stolen his train of thought. This surely had to be one of the interested parties that McCord had warned him about. It wasn't an ordinary burglar because nothing ordinary was missing. He tried to calm himself and think this through. When had he last worked on this? Yesterday afternoon, when he couldn't settle. He had paced back and forth, wandered around the house trying to get focussed. But what exactly had he done? Could he retrace his movements? Lane stood up and followed his memory through the rooms. He had left the study and gone into the lounge. The sun had been coming through the patio door. He had thought that it might help to sit here. He could at least continue reading in the book. That was it! He had put the floppy disk into the book as a bookmark and taken the book through to the lounge. Then what? He still was having trouble concentrating. He had tried unsuccessfully to read the book and then placed the disk back into the book to mark he page…and then what? He scoured his memory. He had picked up the newspaper as a diversion. That was it! He had found an article of interest and decided to save the paper. The book with the disk had gone inside the paper and been taken back into the study. His heart was racing as he moved back to the study. He looked on the desk again. The paper was there. He grabbed it, opened it, and the book and disc were there. He couldn't believe his luck. A huge sense of relief surged through him. His intruder had not found it; he still had it. The guy would never have thought to look inside a folded newspaper. He was sorry now he had taken the newspapers to task earlier in the day; at least they were good for something. Still, some one had identified him as involved in this crazy project. But who?

A little later, when his heart had slowed down a little, Lane went next door and rang Alison's doorbell. She came to the door. 'Oh hi, Davis, come in,' she said.

'Sorry, Alison, I can't come in just now,' he said. 'I just wanted to let you know that it looks like I've had an intruder—that guy you thought was a window cleaner. I think he got in through the bedroom window.'

Alison put her hand up to her mouth. 'Oh Davis, I'm sorry. I should have challenged him when I saw him. Has he taken much?'

'No,' said Lane, 'not as far as I can see. The house is okay, and I can't see that anything is missing. I don't know what he was after.'

'Have you called the police?' Alison asked.

'Not yet,' Lane answered. 'I probably will once I can figure out exactly what happened.' He knew very well that he couldn't call the police. For one thing, he couldn't explain to them about his clandestine project and what the intended theft had been. For another, he couldn't prove beyond a shadow of a doubt that anyone had been in the house, and he didn't want to look the fool. There were no real signs except for a slightly lowered blind. You couldn't expect the police to take that seriously. 'No, I think that everything is OK,' he said, 'Now, let's fix a date for you to come over for dinner. What about Friday night?'

Alison hesitated: 'Are you sure? After all this upset, you might not feel like going to the trouble.'

'No problem,' he answered. Why had he said that? He hated that saying. He hated it when you asked for something in a shop and they said 'no problem.' Anyway, he did have a problem now. 'Come on Friday night about eight. Just be warned that I don't have two Michelin rosettes to my name.' He said it as cheerfully as he could, but he didn't feel at all cheerful.

CHAPTER 13

▼

Back in his own house, Lane poured himself a Lagavulin and settled down in a chair to think. He hadn't wanted to let on to Alison, but he was rattled. Who had been in the house, assuming they had been? He couldn't be absolutely sure about this. Alison certainly had seen someone at the window, and he didn't think that he had left the blind in the study down that far. On the other hand, nothing in the house was disturbed or missing. He had to guess that whoever it was had gone into the study, pulled the blind down so as not to be seen, and tried to find his work on the pc. In this effort, luckily, they had failed. But surely it was clear that whoever it was had targeted Lane as being involved with Clan Caledonia. Moreover, they knew where he lived and now possessed an idea of how he was working. If they hadn't succeeded in getting what they wanted today, they would surely be back.

But in the larger context, when more logic had filtered into his thought, he felt that there were too many unknowns to solve this peculiar equation. He thought he knew what agency he was working for, but he couldn't be absolutely sure. He didn't know who was trying to appropriate his analysis and conclusions, or even if they actually existed in reality. This was a ridiculous position to be in. Why in a secular world should he be victimized for only doing a little theology? The feel-good factor engendered on the loch had completely vanished. He put a CD on and searched for a particular track. It was Rhonda Vincent once again: *Caught in the Crossfire*. Different context but the same problem. He was in range now, right in the middle of the crossfire. He poured himself a second dram. It wasn't because he was worth it; it was because he needed it.

Lane wandered into the study and went online. When he opened up his mailbox there was an email from Katriona:

Dear D:

How are you? I haven't received anything from you lately. Are you OK?

I had a great weekend. Suzy (She's another SW from the States) and I hired a car and drove to Chichicastenango. Everyone here just says Chichi. It's about 2 hours from here. It really is a great place. The scenery on the way is stunning. I know that you would really like it. There's a lake called Atitlan kind of set between two volcanoes. It is very spectacular.

The centre of Chichi town is near Santo Thomas Church. All kinds of rituals seem to be performed there. The people make an offering of copal (not sure what it is), and burn it right in front of the church. So the whole area is filled with smoke and incense. I kept wondering what would happen if we had suggested that at your old charge!

On Sunday they have this wondewrful market! The clothes are fantastic. (Yes, before you say it, I bought a little something). They are great weavers, and the colours of the garments are just stunning. But the fruits and vegetables are wonderful as well. We had a great time just wandering around. The people (genuine Maya, most of them) are so friendly. It was great to get away from G. City for a while and all the problems.

But I do wish you were here!!!

Love,

K.XXX

He read it and then read it again more carefully to try to extract the sights and sounds and smells from her letter. He was envious. It was so ironic—here was Katriona having a great time in a country that he had always pictured as a little dangerous. She was enjoying the scenery, wandering around the town among friendly people, and sampling the wares of the marketplace. And here he was, caught in the crossfire between concealed combatants in some clandestine exercise in Fife of all places! He thought about having another dram and rejected the idea. Instead, he put on another CD and listened until he was falling asleep in the chair. He pulled himself up and went to bed.

When Lane got up the next morning he already knew what he had to do, having lain awake thinking about it since four forty-four. Why was it he so often woke up precisely at four forty-four? Was this supposed to be an important number for him? But it was another number he required. He found the card with Robert McCord's mobile number. After all, the man had said to get in touch him if there was a serious problem. What had happened yesterday would surely constitute a serious problem. He dialled the number and waited. Finally, a recorded message invited him to leave his own message in the voice mailbox. 'Oh great,' he thought, 'this is just what I don't need. Even the CIA doesn't have real people to speak to callers. Next thing you know they'll be using a call centre in India.' He left a message asking for a return call without using his name or telephone number. Surely McCord would recognize the voice.

By eleven his call had not been returned. He was restless and uneasy. There was only one thing to do next. Lane got into the PT Cruiser and headed towards Edinburgh. It was raining again, and the bridge was busy. Why was it busy at this time? There never seemed to be any logic to the traffic these days. If he could figure out some overall pattern to the traffic in order to predict it he could make a million. The traffic eased off once he crossed the bridge.

He went straight along Ferry Road into Leith, and then into Constitution Street. It took ten minutes to find a parking place. He bought a parking ticket for an hour; he couldn't afford to be hassled by a traffic warden just now. In the office of Clan Caledonia, the same receptionist in the same tartan jacket was at her desk scanning *Hello* magazine. There was no one else in the reception area. She looked up when he came in, but showed no signs of recognition.

'Hi,' he said. 'I'm Davis Lane. I was in seeing Mr. McCord some time ago. You may remember.'

She looked unmoved by this disclosure. Eventually her face showed some signs of life. 'Oh,' she said, 'you're the...what was it now? The theology man or something.'

'Yes,' Lane said, 'that's me. I'm actually a freelance theologian.'

'What can I do for you?' the woman asked. 'Is it about an order?' She picked up an arch-file and opened it.

'No, it's not about an order,' Lane replied. 'I need to see Robert McCord pretty urgently. Is he here at the moment?'

'I'm sorry,' she said. 'He isn't. He had to make a trip back to the States. He left yesterday.'

'Great,' said Lane. 'He's in the States? Is there some way I can reach him? I really need to talk to him.'

'Well, I'll tell him that you called if he does ring in. I'll tell him to get in touch right away. Does he have your number?'

'Yes,' said Lane. 'He's got my number. It seems like everybody has my number.' There was no response to this. Her face remained a blank. Had this woman undergone a charisma bypass? Lane turned to walk out the door. When he glanced back, she had put her order file away and was deeply engrossed in *Hello* again. He didn't bother to say goodbye.

Lane sat in the car for a few minutes trying to figure out what to do next. Up until yesterday, he had enjoyed a certain sense of security because of the reassuring presence of Robert McCord. Now he didn't even have that. McCord was not here, and he hadn't indicated that he would be out of the country. Even the presumed fact of his CIA agency was now in question as far as Lane could see. McCord could actually be working for anybody as far as he knew. He sighed and drummed his fingers on the Cruiser's steering wheel. This was a fine mess, and he was stupid for getting into it. After all, he possessed several higher degrees and was supposed to be an intelligent man.

After several minutes, Lane pulled out of his parking space and drove along Constitution Street looking for a place to turn around. He noted a white Mercedes in his rear view mirror. Nice car, lots of style and power, wide sneering grill. He finally had to turn into a side street and then re-enter Constitution Street going in the other direction. Several hundred yards down the way he noted the Merc again in the mirror. This had to be a coincidence, didn't it? He turned left along Bernard Street and passed Clan Caledonia. The Mercedes remained in the mirror. He turned left again and drove up alongside the water of Leith. The Mercedes stayed several hundred yards behind. He turned left again and then right on Leith Walk. There was no mistaking it now; the Merc was tailing him. It was several cars back, but it was there. It looked like there were two people in the car. His heart was beating fast again. Who were these guys and what did they want?

Lane's mind went into first gear, revving hard to figure out what to do next. Where could he go? How could he lose them? It was hard to concentrate on your own driving when someone was following you. He drove all the way up Leith Walk, trying to judge the lights in the hope the Merc might hit a red. It didn't work. He went left at the roundabout at the top of Leith Street and stopped for the red light at Princes Street. Where to next? He took it slowly along Princes Street, hoping that the lights might favour him this time. No luck. Then they were past the Scott Monument, heading west. Lane slowed down for the green at the National Gallery, thinking it might change to red, but it stayed green. The Merc was still two cars behind now, relentlessly on his tail. He was trying hard to think as he drove into the bus pollution zone on Princes Street. There were four or five buses end to end; Princes Street was more like a bus station than the actual station was. He moved into the left-hand lane when he got past the buses. He was approaching the West End now. What next? He signalled left; he would turn into Lothian Road. The Merc followed. They were both around the corner. Then at last, an idea came: The car park—Castle Terrace Car park. They might not want to follow him there. It would be too obvious. He turned left and then left again into the car park. The Merc slowed and pulled into the curb. He rolled down the window, punched the button and took his ticket. He drove quickly down three floors and found a place to park. The Merc was not behind him, thank God. But what to do next? If they were serious, this was not the place to meet them. Who didn't remember the shadows of the D.C. car park where Deep Throat had done his talking. Maybe coming here was a mistake. Lane got out of the car, locked it and exited via the ground-level exit. He crossed the road and entered Princes Street Gardens, looking behind him every few steps. He could hang around the amusement centre for a while. There were people there, and it would at least give him a breather in order to think.

Lane crossed the railway bridge and walked past the fountain. There was no one behind him, at least no one who looked like hit men. He circled past the merry-go-round and tried to look through it: flying horses and children, but no one menacing so far. He sat on a park bench for a while. He could see no one who might be the guys in the Merc. His heart had slowed down and he was beginning to think more clearly. There were two exits to the car park, one at the upper level and one at the lower. They might not know that. They couldn't watch both exits unless one of the guys went there on foot. Even if they used mobile phones it would still take time for the driver to collect his pal. So it might work. It was a gamble, but he would take it.

After an hour, Lane walked back to the car park. He paid at the pay point, extracted his ticket and walked slowly back to the car. There was no sign of them. He got into the car, reversed and headed down the ramp. He would go out the lower exit. At the exit, the ticket went into the machine, the arm lifted, and Lane held his breath as he emerged onto the street, looking both ways. There was no sign of the Merc. The trouble was, of course, that this was now a one-way street. If they were waiting at the end of the street as it came into the Grassmarket, he would be in deep trouble. He drove cautiously, but was ready to pick up speed at any point. The PT Cruiser seemed even more conspicuous now. This was the very time when he needed a low profile. At the corner of the Grassmarket there was still no sign of them. Thank God again. He drove out, but turned left just in case. He could take Victoria Street and come out onto the George IV Bridge. He might escape yet.

Lane drove home as fast as he could, constantly checking his rear-view mirror. The white Merc did not appear, but he was by now genuinely scared. Robert McCord, his sole contact, had disappeared. Someone posing as a window cleaner had broken into his house, searching for information. And now two guys had tailed him halfway across the city. This was no joke. He would have to come to grips with this situation. 'O God, I'm a theologian, not a spy,' he thought to himself. It wasn't a curse; it was a prayer.

When Lane got home he started immediately on the garage. It had never been fully clear since they moved house. He piled the unopened boxes high at the back, and shifted his tools and workbench and the ladder to make more space. He cleaned his bike, oiled the chain and pumped up the tyres. He hadn't used it much, but now was the time. After two solid hours of working, the PT Cruiser slid into the garage. It might help if he were not so obvious. He went inside, poured himself a whisky and dropped into a chair. At least he had made a start. More things would happen in the morning.

CHAPTER 14

▼

The next morning Lane was awake and up early. He ate breakfast, cleared up the kitchen and sat down at the pc. This was the time to be rational and very deliberate. It was not the time to panic. He needed to reconnoiter, to figure out what was happening here. The events of yesterday had been a second wakeup call. He had always believed that it was important to use the reason that God had provided. It was true, of course that you could never reason your way to God. The philosophers had tried that one, but it hadn't worked. The first step always had to be the step of faith, but after that step came reason. On the wall of his study, Lane had pinned up the hand-written reminder he had fashioned years ago. It was now faded and its corners were drooping, but it was still valid. Bill Clinton might have had: *It's the Economy, Stupid*, but he had: *FISOU*. It meant Faith in Search of Understanding. Your faith was always on the lookout for more knowledge, for more understanding of God and the world. You weren't really committed unless you were prepared to think yourself out of the faith. Too many people, especially the more evangelical of whatever religion, didn't always use their reason in thinking things through. And Lane believed that once you had thought things through as carefully as possible, then the systematic pursuit of the implications was important.

He began to type in a summary of what he knew so far. McCord had employed him to research the book, implying that he was acting on behalf of the CIA. But now McCord had left town, disappeared as far as that was concerned. Someone unknown to him had been in the house searching for his work, he assumed. And yesterday two men in a white Merc had tailed him from Leith to the centre of the city. For what purpose?

Lane walked to the kitchen and got himself another cup of coffee. He drank it looking out of the window. It was a nice day. He should really be outside lapping up some sunshine. Instead of that he was stuck in the house trying to penetrate this murky situation.

When he sat down at the pc again and studied what he had on the monitor, it all seemed too ambiguous. He didn't know if McCord really worked for the CIA or some other agency. He could be MI5 or even an agent of the Washington hawks. Moreover, now he had disappeared. He could simply be on a business trip to the States. Maybe Langley had summoned him back urgently. He wasn't absolutely certain that someone had been in the house. It was true that Alison had seen someone at the window, but that didn't mean the guy had broken in. It could have been a different window cleaner attacking the windows of the wrong house. The guys in the Merc certainly seemed to tail him, but could that have been a coincidence? There were too many unknowns in this equation. The line between fact and his imagination was becoming too thin. The only solution, if you could call it that, was to continue working but at a faster rate. Get through the thing. Get it over with. At the same time, he would need to be more careful about leaving the house and about watching his back.

Lane returned to studying the book, reading each day's devotion, underlining the key points and making notes. The trouble with Chambers was that no clear-cut guidelines to the Christian life ever really emerged. It looked as if he were going to tell you something important, something you could get your teeth into, but the bottom line always receded into the believer's private relationship with God and Christ. It was like casting for trout imperfectly. The action of the arm seemed right, the line snaked back, but on the forward movement it didn't loop out to land the flies gently on the water. Somewhere in mid-air, the cast got hung up. So also, in Chambers' theology, any concrete advice to the Christian got hung up in the atmosphere of growing more intimate with God.

Lane worked another hour on the book and then put it aside. It was tedious, and he was near to dozing off on some pages. He would need to change the pace for a while in order to wake up. He saved the notes he had made and extracted the floppy disk. He placed the floppy disk in the hollow base of the globe he kept on top of the file cabinet. It wasn't likely that anyone would think to look there. He squeezed the book in beside a row of other paperbacks on the bookshelf. He had so many books lined up that it would take anyone an age to find this one. He hoped that he could find it again himself.

Lane went out through the back door, having made certain that the bedroom window was closed and the doors securely locked. He extracted his bike from the garage and headed up the coastal path towards Aberdour. The sun was shining on the waters of the Forth, the air was warm, and there were cyclists and walkers on the path. It struck him that his present inactivity was crazy. Other people were out enjoying the natural world, but he was stuck in the study living dangerously. He must be getting paranoid.

It was good to ride again, but he was still a little shaky. It wasn't completely true what people said about bicycles—that once you had learned to ride you never lost the skill. Certainly you remembered how to ride, but it wasn't with quite the same confidence. Threading between boulders and gates along the path was done slowly and with anxiety. When he was young he could ride without his hands on the handlebars; he wouldn't dare try that now. He rode past the rusty pier and the old quarry and then alongside the beach towards Dalgety Bay. A blonde in jeans was throwing stones for her black lab on the beach. The dog raced after each stone, raising little clouds of sand behind each foot. It carefully smelled the stones to locate the one that had been thrown, gingerly lifted it and then dutifully returned it to drop it at its mistress's feet. It must be wonderful to be made so happy by something as simple as a tossed stone! The costal path had now been completed around the new houses at St David's; it made life easier for the cyclists. Then he rode up the hill, along past Donibristle House and the sailing club, the most historic stretch of this area. Between the Bay and Aberdour, the path ran through fields, allowing unrestricted views of the Forth. Inchcolm Island with its priory loomed large in the water this morning, and it was clear enough to see Granton all the way across the Forth. This was the bit he always enjoyed the most. Nearing Aberdour, the path ran through large old beech trees that bordered the golf course on the right. It was really beautiful, and he was beginning to feel better again.

When Lane reached Aberdour, he spotted Melvin's Mobile Barbershop in the station parking lot. He might as well have a word with Melvin before having a pub lunch. He leaned the bike against the side of the bus and went up the steps. Melvin was snipping away at the hair of a small boy on the child's seat of the chair. The boy was rigid in the chair; probably his first haircut, Lane thought.

'Hey, Mr. Lane,' Melvin said when Lane stepped through the door. 'How are you? Do you need another cut already?'

'I'm fine,' Lane answered. 'I haven't come for a haircut, though. I just saw the bus and thought I would say hello.'

Melvin was brushing hair off the boy's face and asking his mum if the cut was all right. When she paid and the two left, he motioned for Lane to sit down. As there were no other customers waiting. Melvin climbed up into the barber's chair and swung it around to face Lane.

'I'm doing OK,' Melvin said. 'Business could be better, but I can't complain. Hey, did your friends find you?'

Lane sat up straighter and studied him. 'Sorry? What do you mean?'

'Your two friends,' said Melvin. 'They were here last week and looking for you.'

'Who were they?' Lane asked.

'How should I know that?' Melvin said. 'Only the one guy got his haircut. The other guy just waited. They asked if I had seen you lately. Said they were friends of yours.'

'What did they look like?' Lane asked.

'What did they look like? How am I supposed to remember how they looked? They're your friends.'

'But I don't know who you are talking about, Melvin. I haven't had the chance to make many friends in the Kingdom of Fife. What were they driving?'

'I have no idea,' said Melvin. 'Look, these two guys came into the shop. They're wearing suits. I don't get many people in suits, you know. One of them wants a haircut. The other guy just sits and looks at the *Daily Record*. The guy getting the haircut is all chatty. He asks me if I know Davis Lane. I say, "Sure, Mr. Lane comes in all the time. He is one of my best customers. He talks more than most people, but that's all right.' Melvin smiled and winked at Lane. 'He asked me how you were doing, how was your work going?'

Lane jumped in: 'What did you say?'

'I said that you were OK. I said that you were talking theology as usual, passing me your weird ideas, that now you were saying that God wasn't all-powerful, that he couldn't do everything. Is that right? Is that what you said?'

Lane nodded. 'Yes, that'll do. What else did he say?'

'Not much. He didn't seem all that interested. He wondered where you lived, said they'd like to look in and see you.'

'What did you say?' Lane asked, increasingly anxious now.

'Hey, how should I know where you live? I don't bring the bus to you. You come to the bus. I told him I thought you lived somewhere in Inverkeithing. That was it; they went away. The guy didn't even give me a tip. I guess they didn't find you, eh?'

'No, they didn't,' Lane replied, but he wasn't at all sure. Lane said goodbye to Melvin and stepped down from the bus. He collected the bike and walked it slowly back towards the coastal path. His heart was racing again. He wouldn't go for lunch today; something else had captured his attention: who were these guys?

CHAPTER 15

▼

Lane cycled home as fast as his lack of skill and the coastal path would permit. But his anxiety about the house was groundless; it was fine. All the doors were secure, as were the windows. His working disk was still at the bottom of the world and the book was still tucked away on the shelf. He sighed audibly with relief. But this latest alarm only made the puzzle harder to solve. Were the two men who turned up at Melvin's bus the same two who had tailed him in the white Merc? Perhaps, but he couldn't be sure. If only Melvin had been able to see their car. Clearly, they had wanted to find out where he lived. It was fortunate that the Lane's name and address had not yet appeared in the telephone directory. But over and above that, what did they want?

Lane sat at the desk trying once again to think things through. He was aware that this was becoming a habit. He was spending more time trying to figure things out than in doing anything else. He had to do something to fit these various pieces of the jigsaw into place. He remembered the telephone number that McCord had given him before. The implication was that it was the number for the CIA in Langley. Lane looked up the area code for Langley, Virginia and dialled. Sure enough, the recorded message said that this was the headquarters of the Central Intelligence Agency. The automated answering service came as a shock; it could be the gas board or the bank or any of the other ordinary institutions that one had to deal with every day. The voice then went on to say that if you wanted this or that department you should press this or that number. What if you were trying urgently to report a terrorist plot: For the terrorist bomb department, press 6? But there was no department for overseas surveillance. There was a number that promised to connect you with a real, live person, but

Lane reckoned they would deny any knowledge of an agent McCord in Edinburgh. Moreover, if McCord was not a CIA agent, the department would be very interested, and that carried the potential to deepen Lane's dilemma. He hung up. He would mull it over for a while.

Several hours later, having made rather feeble gestures at tidying the house, Lane was no further forward at assembling the jigsaw. He switched on the television and sat down. Perhaps there would be something that would distract him, take his mind off the ever-deepening situation. He scanned through the programmes without discovering anything that grabbed him. It was incredible to think that with a hundred channels or more there was nothing that appealed. He finally settled on a nature channel. But he could get only half-involved. The mind kept going back to window cleaners and white Mercs and two men who pretended to be friends and asked questions. The problem was that he had not been able to share any of these experiences. They were tumbling about in his mind without any external sorting system to help order them. In spite of what McCord had said, he would really need to talk to someone. He phoned Allen.

The Reverend Dr. Allen Mutch was a friend, of sorts. He was a parish minister in Edinburgh and had been in place in his church and parish even before Lane had been inducted to his charge. He must be, Lane pondered, now well into his seventies. Having been inducted to his charge before a certain date he was *ad vitam aut culpam*. The designation meant that he could stay in his parish for the whole of his life or until mortal sin intervened. It suited Allen to stay where he was, even though the congregation had greatly dwindled over the years. Allen was really more the academic type. He had gained a Master's degree at Union Seminary in New York and had been given several honorary degrees over the years. In fact, Allen was so heavily degree-ed that Lane suspected he promoted himself solely for that purpose. He seemed to enjoy receiving honours as other people enjoyed ill health. He didn't spend much time labouring in the parish, so it gave him lots of opportunities to work in the library.

At Union Theological Seminary in New York, Allen had studied under Reinhold Niebuhr, the great American theologian. The Niebuhr influence was still strong, so when it came to theology and ethics, Allen was a realist. In Lane's opinion, he was one of the few Church of Scotland ministers who still thought theologically. Allen T. Mutch was a peculiar mix. He had a quick mind, which made him good in debate in the presbytery and General Assembly. He was adept at thinking on his feet in the heat of debate. But his interjections often prolonged debate without providing significant development. The fact that Allen had never revealed what his middle initial stood for gave scope to his colleagues in this respect. When Allen rose to speak, other ministers and elders were often heard to sigh and mutter under their breath, 'Oh no, it's Too Much again.'

Lane's friendship with Mutch had always been slightly ambivalent. The man was very critical of many of his colleagues. When the two of you conversed, you both stood head and shoulders over everyone else in the church, yet the feeling persisted that in his very next conversation with someone else you might be subject to the same kind of fierce criticism. But Mutch's worst vitriol was always aimed at the administrators at the church headquarters at 121 George Street, known to everyone simply as "121". For Allen, many of the staff them were simply buffoons. For him they were incompetent and were merely serving their own interests rather than the interests of the whole church.

Because of his persistent but largely accurate critical forays, Allen had long since been marginalized. The establishment tried its best to ignore him and succeeded. Whereas some other ministers attracted attention and praise by virtue of their family connections or their well-practiced ability to make friends and influence people, Allen—in spite of his intellect-was pushed beyond the pale. He claimed that he had long since given up caring, but it was obvious that deep down he was smouldering.

He did a little work in his parish, preached on Sundays and spent the rest of the time in the library writing books. Lane could hardly count him as a good friend because Allen was so volcanic. Watching the eruption was spectacular, yet you were always afraid that you might also be swept away by the flow of acid. But Lane respected Mutch's theological and ecclesiastical insight. He also felt sorry for the man. The irony was that someone with so much to offer to the church could be so easily relegated to the margins because of his critical faculties. Jean, his wife of fifty years, had unquestionably saved Allen many times. She was warm and kindly, somehow always healing the wounds that Allen had inflicted. She visited members, invited them to the manse for scones and coffee and kept the channels of communication open.

Lane felt that Mutch's knowledge and insight were unsurpassed. If anyone might be able to help him fit some of the pieces together, it would be Allen. But by exactly the same token, he had to be careful, for giving away too much to the man wasn't always safe. His tirades about the faults of institutions and other people had been known to lead him betray a confidence.

When Lane had called Allen last night, he had said that he would be working in the National Library of Scotland. He suggested that they meet for coffee at the National Museum of Scotland, just around the corner on Chambers Street. Lane was meticulous about leaving the house now. The disk and book were safely stowed away, the windows and doors locked. He rode the bike up to the station and locked it to the railings, crossed the tracks and waited for the nine thirty-five to Edinburgh. From Waverley Station he climbed the long flight of steps up past the Bank of Scotland headquarters. He hated these steps. For one thing, they reminded him that he was unfit. For another, one or two guys with blankets pulled up to their chins were always spread out on these steps holding out their polystyrene cups for money. They usually had their dogs peeking out from under the blanket as well, looking just as mournful. Lane wondered how they had trained their dogs to be beggars. Some people trained their dogs to be bird dogs, others to be guide dogs for the blind. These guys trained their dogs to be beggars. He was as compassionate as anyone else, but he didn't think they were genuinely in need. They were probably better off than him. At least the guys who sold the Big Issue were trying. He was glad when he reached the top of the steps; it wasn't far down over George IV Bridge to the museum.

As Lane wound his way through the revolving door of the museum he spotted the familiar figure of Allen Mutch at the far end of the room. Allen appeared to be studying the Millennium Clock as it celebrated the hour. The clock was an amazing assemblage of gears and chains and revolving figures. Mutch was thin and tall with a slight stoop. He was mostly bald now, but sported an immaculately trimmed white beard. He always wore a tweed suit and deerstalker cap and always carried a briefcase and umbrella. Lane had never seen him dressed in any other way or without the briefcase and umbrella. Half-frame spectacles under steely grey eyes completed the academic look. Mutch stuck out his hand and greeted Lane enthusiastically.

'Davis, good to see you. Are you well?' Mutch said. Without pausing for an answer, he went on. 'The reason I suggested that we meet here was that I wanted to see this new exhibition.'

'What exhibition is that?' Lane asked, suddenly realizing that his project had cut him off from what was happening in the rest of the world. He turned his head to see if he could spot something to provide a clue to what Mutch was talking about. The museum was busy and most of the tables in the new café were occupied.

'It's the "Fuzzy Raptor" exhibit,' Mutch answered.

'The what?' Lane asked.

'The Fuzzy Raptor Exhibit,' Mutch answered. 'It's really called "Dino Birds". It's about the evolution of dinosaurs into winged and feathered creatures with the potential to fly. They have discovered fossils of these things in China.' Mutch led them towards a door in the middle of the south wall. They stopped at the desk to buy tickets and went through the door.

'I didn't know that ~~know~~ you were interested in fossils,' Lane volunteered, smiling. Mutch was studying one of the photographs of fuzzy raptors on the wall. He looked at Lane and broke into a mischievous grin.

'Well, you have to be if you minister in the Church of Scotland, don't you?'

Lane wasn't sure that he had heard the man correctly; the place was noisy, full of school kids running around with notebooks and pencils.

'Haven't you heard about the Fuzzy Raptor?' Allen asked.

'No,' Lane replied. 'I seem to be out of touch with nearly everything these days.'

'This is the missing link,' said Mutch. 'They've always speculated that birds evolved from dinosaurs. Well, these fossils might be the link. They had little wings with feathers but didn't fly as such. They think that these little dinos used their feathered wings to help them run faster on the ground. They flapped their wings in order to pick up speed, but in doing so they accidentally created enough lift to get off the ground. They then gradually learned to fly. That's why I think there is a lesson here for the church. If it doesn't begin to run fast and flap its wings like hell it will soon be like the dinosaurs—dead and gone.' Lane was plunged into a fit of laughing.

As they moved around the exhibit, Lane studied the fossils embedded in the stone slabs. He could make out the wings and long legs and could imagine how evolution might have taken place. It was interesting, but he had other things on his mind.

'It is fascinating right enough,' he said. 'So, Allen, how are you and how is Jean?' he asked when the older man finally looked up from the case.

'Well, apart from the usual aches and pains, I'm OK There is no use of complaining, Davis. No use at all. Nobody listens to you. But Jean's fine. She's entertaining several of the Guild today.' The two men found a seat in a space that was designed for rest and reflection. On another bench several of the kids in school uniform were making sketches in their spiral notebooks.

Lane thought to himself that Allen had complained so often in his life that it was no wonder people didn't listen. 'I know what you mean,' he answered. Lane noted that Allen did not ask him how he was. He never had. Funny how unilateral relationships could be sometimes. 'What are you working on now?' he asked.

'Ach, it's just a wee book about the future of the Church of Scotland. I've got some money from a source to publish it.' Allen was adept at scouting around to find money to support his various projects. He knew about every trust fund that ever existed.

'Does the Church have a future?' Lane asked. 'The rate at which it's declining and the shortage of ministers—it's looks to me as if it will collapse in the near future.'

'Davis,' Mutch said, slapping his knee and clearly warming to the question, 'If only it would collapse. If only the General Assembly would acknowledge that there is a real crisis and the media could focus on it, then we might be able to do something to halt the decline. But it won't happen like that. All that happens is that the church shrinks year by year. Finances decline, programmes—the most creative ones—are cut. One of these days the General Assembly will consist of a committee of twelve balding men huddled around the Moderator's chair on the Mound. The Church will go out not with a bang, but with a whimper.'

'You're probably right,' said Lane. 'But who do you blame? There are some good people doing their best to renew the church.'

'Davis, I know that,' said Mutch. 'You did a good job in your church, and there are ministers and elders in various places who are really committed, unlike lots of our colleagues in the ministry who only think about what furthers their career. But it's the guys at 121 who really make me angry. The boards and agencies operate as independent units; the one doesn't know what the other is doing and doesn't care. Each one is trying to carve out its own little kingdom. Nobody gives a damn about the whole church. And they've got people there, lawyers most of them, who don't know their elbows from their asses, pardon my language. They get so hung up on church law that the Church slides down the slope right under their noses. Talk about straining out a gnat and swallowing a camel. These people are adept at straining and swallowing. Straining and swallowing: it's become a way of life for them. Davis, I'm sick of it, really sick of it.' Mutch was agitated now, gesturing at the large picture of Archaeopteryx as if it were 121 George Street.

Lane started to say something about his own problems but was interrupted by Mutch. 'You know, Davis. The Church of Scotland is more like an old boys club than a community of saints. If your name is McSomething, or if your grandfather and father were ministers, or if you come from a line of theologians whether good or bad, then you can do no wrong. The General Assembly will lie prostrate in order to hear every last pearl that drops from your mouth. It doesn't matter whether you have anything useful or creative to say or not, you will be heard and go far. But if you don't have a Scottish pedigree or if you have something creative to say and you are even a little critical of the establishment, bingo. That's it; they

some Christians who are ready to follow Leviticus to the hilt: crush the balls of the sinners, stone the adulterers. We have to accept that these attitudes are real and deal with them on that basis. We can't keep going around and saying 'Let's sit down and have a little dialogue over tea, shall we? Oh excuse me, you can't drink tea, can you?'

'Yes, I agree with you,' said Lane. 'I think that so many people now have been turned off to violence by actually seeing it on the news, that they believe evil can be made to disappear, like magic: Come in Harry Potter. They think that by merely thinking good and noble thoughts we can bring an end to injustice and violence. They don't see that sometimes you have to have the courage to dirty your own hands to achieve something that is good and right. The trouble is now that we are bereft of the kind of great theologians of the past who provided guidance and leadership. Like Martin Luther, for example. Remember that Luther said we had to sin bravely.'

Mutch responded, 'Of course, and Bonhoeffer saw the nature of the Third Reich and got involved in the plot to kill Hitler.'

'Exactly,' Lane said, 'and coming back to Reinhold Niebuhr, did Niebuhr not get the States to go to war against the Third Reich?'

'Absolutely,' Mutch answered. 'He also influenced a whole generation of political scientists. In those days everyone listened to him, the politicians and even the economists. He clarified the nature of the world because he was a realist. What theologian today can you name that anyone listens to?'

'I can't,' said Lane, trying to think of a Scottish theologian of influence. 'If you go into the bookshop to look for some good theological work, all you get are spiritual books, super sweet volumes of inspirational crap. It's so depressing. But listen, Allen, what do you make of my situation?'

'I don't think you're in any danger,' Mutch answered. 'I think they just want to get their hands on your analysis.'

'Is that all?' asked Lane.

Mutch was silent for a moment, thinking. 'No, I suppose not. It can't be all there is to it. They wouldn't go to such lengths only for that, would they? There are other people who could give them an analysis of Oswald Chambers.' Lane supposed that Allen might even be thinking of himself.

'Exactly,' said Lane. The thought had roamed vaguely around his mind, but he had been unable to put it in so many words. 'So why me.'

'There has to be something else,' said Mutch. 'Something else they think you have or are going to get.'

This was a new idea to Lane. He hadn't thought of that before. 'But what?' he asked.

Mutch looked at him reflectively. 'I don't know.'

'Neither do I,' Lane said.

Lane walked with Mutch back to the National Library and then headed back to the station. The train coming in from Fife was late as usual. On the way home he tried to think clearly about why he was being watched, followed, invaded, whatever. It was hard to be relaxed under these circumstances. His conversation with Allen might have clarified things to some degree, but it hadn't really provided much comfort. From the rail bridge he could see the red and white Superfast Ferry heading down the Forth towards Zeebrugge. The passengers would be feeling good by now, enjoying the view of the bridges and having a drink. He wished he and Katriona were on it. He wished he were anywhere but here.

CHAPTER 16

▼

When he went online the next morning there was an email from Katriona.

Dear D:

Please, please, please send me an email and tell me what you are doing and if you are all right! I haven't gotten anything from you in days. I was beginning to wonder if my email was working, but I have had messages from other people. You don't have to write a book. Just let me know that you are OK.

I've been working all hours lately and am really tireed. But it does feel good to know that you are helping people who appreciate it. We had a sad case yesterday. A boy was in a dumpster searching, apparently on his own. He either didn't hear the truck r4eversing to lift it or he was afraid to try and get out. Anyway, the dumpster was lifted and dumped with him in it. He had no chance. I've been trying to comfort hgis mother, but its really hard. She has no idea where his father is.

Because of the trip to Chichi I'm worried a little about money. I spent more than I should have. Sorry! Do you think that you could send a little to me. If it's too difficult, don't worry.

Please let me hear from you.

Love,

K.XXX

Lane sent a reply:

Dear K:

Sorry, sorry, sorry. I've been very busy and just lost track of the time. I'm fine, working hard but enjoying my project. I've had to do quite a lot of running about. Yesterday I meant Allen in the museum. He was asking for you. He and Jean are fine.

Please don'ty work so hard that you get exhausted. This is supposed toi be something different from the normal routine!

No problem about the money. I'll try to send some today. Just let me know when you are running low. I'll phone you soon for a real chat.

Love,

D.XXX

After sending the mail, Lane sat at his desk for a while, trying to put some order into the scrambled pieces of information and obligation that were circulating around his brain. He would have to get back to Katriona in a more substantial way and let her know that he would arrange to send her money. He felt guilty; not only was Katriona trying to get by on a pittance, but she was also dealing with real people and genuine tragedy while he was dealing with a dubious theology and shadowy figures. He would have to make a decision about how to proceed on the Chambers project, shrouded as it was in ambiguity. And he would have to stop being paranoid if he were to accomplish anything at all.

He went over his meeting with Allen Mutch. Allen had reckoned that there had to be something else they were after, whoever they were. Had Lane missed something essential? Was there some other angle to this project he had not seen? Was there something that McCord had deliberately not told him? There seemed to be no obvious answers to these questions. There might be some comfort in Allen's opinion that Lane wasn't in danger, but precious little. Allen hadn't had the Merc tailing him all over the city. Lane wasn't sure if his physical well-being was in danger or not, but his sanity certainly was. He found himself constantly looking over his shoulders these days. He couldn't even leave the house without locking everything up. He hadn't ventured out with the PT Cruiser in days. He was suffering car deprivation. There seemed to be nothing else to do except get back to the book and the analysis, but he would need to finish the thing as soon as possible. It was early in the day, but Lane poured himself a dram—his first in days—and sat down with the book. He put on a CD: The Bob Wills Cowboy Band. Maybe it would give him a laugh and relieve the tension.

But Bob Wills and his band didn't do it this time. It was too light for his mood, too full of bubbles in the beer and San Antonio roses. He needed something heavier or at least something with more tempo to move him along. He tried LeAnn Rimes and found some help in *Nothin' New Under the Moon.*

Lane ploughed again into *My Utmost,* carefully reading each devotion and marking the key passages that gave insight into Chambers' thought. It was hard to understand why this book appealed to so many people around the world. It never seemed to go anywhere beyond the circle of the believer's intimate relationship with God. Perhaps this was precisely why it appealed to people; it placed no real demands on the believer for moral activity in the world. In fact, Lane suddenly realised, it was a very anti-ethical book. In the devotion for June 6, Chambers wrote:

Look to Jesus and you will find that your will and your conscience are in agreement with Him every time.

And later on the same page:

Your natural choices will be in accordance with God's will, and living this life will be as natural as breathing.

So as long as the believer is convinced that he is at one with Jesus his conscience will agree with Jesus, and no moral thought need be given to life. Chambers provided no rules or principles or norms to give guidance to the shape of moral life in the world. Religious conviction would lead automatically to Christian morality. There was no consideration given here to the persistence of sin in every Christian, no reminder of St. Paul's cry of despair:

I do not understand my own actions. For I do not do what I want, but I do the very thing I hate.

No wonder that people were interested in the president's infatuation with this work. It sanctioned any kind of activity you might wish to engage in. Persuasive suggestions in his ear could lead to momentous decisions. True, you were supposed to feel at one with Jesus, but lots of misguided people felt that. Jesus himself had said, 'Not everyone who says to me, "Lord, Lord..."' Lane had no doubt that Oswald Chambers would not have wished his work to be interpreted in this way. The trouble was that life is replete with unintended consequences. Chambers was not concerned enough with the world. Indeed, the work had very little to do with action in the world. It was all about exhibition. The believer is to exhibit his new life in Christ and in this way draw others into the faith. It was a store window kind of faith: dressed in the glow of an intimate relationship with God, the believer appealed to the passers-by. But if they were drawn into the faith, they would probably want to be in the window as well, rather than in the world.

By eleven that night Lane was in bed, mentally exhausted by his day with the book. Just as he was dropping off, the phone rang.

'Hello, Davis?' It was Robert McCord.

'McCord,' he answered. 'Is that you? Where the hell have you been?'

'Let's keep this short,' McCord replied. 'Don't mention anything specific, names or places. I'm sorry I've been out of touch. I had to make a fast trip to the States. My secretary told me that you came into the office.'

'You're right about that,' Lane said. 'A long time ago. I thought that you had abandoned me. I have things to tell you.'

'Not now, not over the phone,' McCord answered. 'Could we meet up tomorrow for lunch, same place we met the first time?'

'OK, yes. It's essential,' Lane replied. 'Let's make it about twelve.'

'Right,' said McCord. 'Mind how you come though, if you know what I mean.'

'You better believe it,' Lane said with added emphasis. 'See you then.' He hung up, his heart racing. Everything that had happened over the last few days came flooding back into his head. It would be hell getting to sleep now.

CHAPTER 17

▼

He slept badly: not so much dreaming dreams as creating screenplays. Every time he closed his eyes some new and weird scenario would take place on the stage of his semi-consciousness. Each one was more bizarre than the previous one; none of them made sense or made him feel good. Bad nights were beginning to become a habit. By six he had had enough. He got up, shaved and showered and tried to think through the day ahead while having some breakfast. He had not only to figure out how to get to Harry's Bar without being observed but also about how to secure the house and his work. More importantly, he had to recall and replay the events of the last few days for Robert McCord. He was surprised at how much anger was building within him. It was one thing to be rewarded well for doing a job that he enjoyed; it was another thing to be invaded and pursued by agents unknown and to be simultaneously abandoned by the very person who had promised his support. He would need to express all this to McCord. The trouble was that he didn't like getting angry with people.

At seven the phone rang again. It was Katriona: 'Davis, where the hell have you been?' she said.

'I'm sorry,' he answered. 'I did send you an email.'

'Yes, I got that,' Katriona answered. 'But what I said in my email to you was that you didn't have to write a book. I didn't mean that a couple of sentences would do. I just want to know what you are doing and how you are. I'm missing you.'

'I'm missing you too,' he said. 'I know I should have written more. It's just that it is amazingly hectic here. It doesn't seem like there is enough time to do everything. I'll be sending you money today, but don't worry about it. There's plenty in the account.'

'Fine,' she said, 'but it would be nice to talk with you at length. What on earth are you doing? What's making life so hectic? I'm feeling all on my own here. It's fine during the day when there is more than enough work to do, but the evenings are long and lonely.'

'Look,' Lane answered, 'I understand what you mean, but I'll have to go now. I'll ring you tonight and we can have a proper chat.' She agreed somewhat reluctantly to that and they hung up. Why did everything happen at once, he thought to himself? He liked to deal with one thing at a time, and now too many things were competing simultaneously for his full attention.

A little later in the morning Lane carefully put the book in its place on the shelf, hid the disk under the globe and locked all the doors and windows. He headed up to the town centre along the back path, taking a moment now and then to check for strange window cleaners or white Mercedes. At the bank he arranged to send money to Katriona. Even allowing for this transfer, the account was still well in balance; it should be, he thought, there's been no chance to spend money on anything else. He hadn't even bought a new CD in weeks. He ambled casually along the main street, looking into shop windows, not that there were many to look into in Inverkeithing. The wind was whipping along the street this morning, sending plastic bags and chip cartons scooting along the pavement. Just past St Peter's Church he cut to the left down through the station parking lot, then across the disused track and into the station approach road. He bought a ticket for Haymarket, crossed the bridge over the tracks and waited. There was no sign of anyone following him. He hoped that this meeting would clarify things. The questions just wouldn't stop asserting themselves: who was the pseudo window cleaner? Who were the guys in the white Merc, and the two guys in Melvin's barber bus? And for that matter, who was Robert McCord? His initial respect for the man was fast eroding.

McCord was at Harry's before him, wearing a dark trench coat and looking as laid back as ever. Stooping to study the menu on the railing, he looked sideways at Lane, flashed a broad smile and stretched out his hand.

'Davis, good to see you,' he said.

'Yeah, well, I'm surprised to see you,' Lane responded. 'I've been trying to get you for long enough.'

McCord simply said, 'Sorry about that. Let's go get something to eat.'

When the waitress had seated them and taken their orders for drinks, Lane said 'You haven't a clue what I've been through.'

'Well, maybe not or maybe I can guess' said McCord. 'In any event, tell me about it.'

Lane launched into his tale about the window cleaner, the trip to Clan Caledonia and the white Merc, and about the two curious guys at Melvin's. When he was trying to explain to McCord about Melvin and the mobile barbershop, the waitress came back, looking for their order. They apologized and sent her away. Lane found himself going on at full flow with the story until McCord interrupted, suggesting that they decide on what to eat; otherwise the girl would need to be sent away again. They ordered and Lane carried on, putting heavy emphasis on the fact that McCord hadn't been available when required. McCord was attentive, but silent.

'So what do you think?' Lane asked. 'What do you make of it all? And over and above that, where the hell have you been?'

'I'm sorry that you had all that to cope with,' McCord said, looking genuinely aggrieved. 'And I'm sorry that I wasn't around when you needed me.'

Lane took a long drink. He sensed the anger rising again and made no move to check it. 'Yes, why was that?' he asked. 'When I agreed to your proposition you assured me that you would stick with me at every point. When it came right down to it, you weren't there.'

'I know, and I am sorry,' McCord answered. 'But the fact is that there were new developments. I had to go back, like quick, to Langley to get information and take advice. There was no chance to tell you. We didn't know that they would be onto you so quickly.'

'You didn't know that who would be onto me? Lane asked. 'Who are these guys?'

McCord sighed and looked Lane in the eye, a weak smile on his face. 'I have a confession to make to you,' he said.

'O good, a confession,' Lane answered. 'We're getting theological at last. And what might that be?'

'I think I know who's putting the pressure on you, but it takes a bit of explanation. When we were making the case in Langley to get you to do this job, we really had to work at it. Not everyone in the upper echelon of the agency was convinced that it was worth spending money on. We have people who pull the purse strings even there, you know. Anyway, while the department was happy with the goal of the assignment, there was debate about your remuneration. So we had to find a way of justifying it.' McCord looked away and studied the stained glass window in the back wall for a few seconds. He turned back to Lane. 'So, we said that you had special expertise for this task. We said that only you could do the kind of theological analysis that would answer the questions we had.'

'Well, I'm flattered,' Lane said, 'but that isn't true, as you know. There are lots of people who could do what I'm doing and probably do it better. But I wouldn't say that your fabrication was a cardinal sin.'

'No,' McCord broke in, 'but that isn't all. What happened was that somewhere along the line between Edinburgh and Langley, there was a leak. That's why I had to go back—to find out where the leak is and try to plug it. The bottom line is that some other group got the message from us that you are the world expert on Oswald Chambers.'

Lane sat upright in the chair, feeling stunned. 'You're saying that some other intelligence agency has me down for being the only person in the world who can decipher Oswald Chambers?'

'I'm afraid so,' McCord answered, looking decidedly sheepish.

'So that's why I'm being pursued all over the place?' Lane asked.

'Right again,' McCord said.

'So you are saying that I, me, Davis Lane, Freelance Theologian is the Number One Target?'

'Well,' McCord answered, 'let's not overstate the case, but yes. You are pretty high up there.'

'That's wonderful,' Lane said. 'That's just great. You've just put up a target and drawn the bull's-eye right around me.'

'I really am sorry,' McCord replied, 'but we are working on it. We think we know who intercepted the message and is desperate to get their hands on your analysis.'

'So tell me,' Lane asked. 'How do you interpret everything that's happened to me?'

'Well,' McCord answered, 'from what you've said, I suspect that the two guys on the barbershop bus are probably the same two guys who followed you from my office. By the way, I'm not sure it was all that clever going into the car park. What if they had followed you in there? It would have been easy to locate your car, and then they would have had you. In any event, you would have had to pay for your ticket in order to exit. And at that point they would have had you.'

'That's true,' Lane said. 'I hadn't thought of that, but let's face it. I've never been tailed like that before. I only watch this stuff in the movies. Freelance theologians don't usually get followed and threatened, you know. I'm lucky if I can find anyone to be interested in *anything* I do. You're the expert on espionage. How do you expect me to know how to act?'

McCord laughed. 'OK, point well taken. But I'm not sure that they were threatening you.'

'They seemed pretty damn threatening to me,' Lane said. 'All I could see was that ominous Mercedes grill in my mirror.'

'OK, I appreciate that Davis,' McCord said, donning an all too obvious pastoral look.

'Anyway,' Lane replied, 'tell me who you think these guys are.'

'We'll come to that in a minute,' McCord said. 'Can we go back to your window cleaner? Do you think he was for real and that he actually got into your house?'

'My neighbour told me about him,' said Lane. 'He wasn't my regular cleaner, and it looks like he was in the study.'

'Did he get any information from you?' McCord said.

'No, I don't think so, but that was purely by accident.' Lane responded.

'Good,' said McCord. 'But I'm not sure what to make of him. In a way, he worries me more than the two guys or the four guys or whatever. He seems more competent than they are.'

'You seem to take it pretty lightly,' Lane said, still feeling the knot of anger in his stomach. 'I don't like having my home and security invaded by people I don't know.'

'Sorry again,' said McCord. 'It's just so much part and parcel of the game that I guess I take it for granted.'

The waitress brought their food and McCord sat back from the table and studied the other customers. 'I was afraid you might be followed this morning,' he said. 'That's why I didn't want to talk about where we would meet and why I asked you to be careful.'

They began to eat, but McCord ate slowly and deliberately, interweaving the food with conversation, his fork mirroring the main points over his plate. 'You see, when we realised that we had a leak we knew that your position would be precarious. I just didn't think they would be in Edinburgh so soon or I would have found some way to warn you. But it's clear that they are on to what you are doing for us. As to who they are, I can only give you our best guess. I don't think that Mossad believes this issue is that vital. Anyway they have their hands full with Palestinian terrorists at the moment. I think it's possible that MI5 might be on your tail. They are desperate to know the kind of political wasteland that the president might land your prime minister in. My guess is that the window cleaner might be an MI5 man. It was kind of clever, that window cleaning ploy. But the Merc guys and the barbershop bus guys—I think they have to be the same two.

And I would bet that they are working for the neo-conservatives in Washington. The hawks are smart, really smart. They have a very clear agenda—the domination of the world by the United States. It's rather breathtaking when you think about it. They have massive support from the religious right in the country. They think it's the only way to confront Islam and all the other anti-American groups. Their plan is to get inside the president's head by finding out what motivates him. One key thing that motivates him is Oswald Chambers' book. It isn't just *what* Chambers says; it's also *when* he says it. In other words, because the devotions follow the days of the year there may be several particular days when the president is more than ever open to suggestion. And once they're in his head they can manipulate him to fall in with their own agenda. I mean, it is clever. So there you are. That's how I see things.' McCord laid down his knife and fork and picked up the napkin.

'So the two guys are agents of the hawks?' Lane asked.

'Not really agents as such,' McCord said. 'The neo-conservatives don't have a real structure, only a kind of web. It is an informal, very low profile network that they use. So for an operation like this one they have to employ local talent. In this case, the talent they chose looks pretty amateurish to me.'

'So you're saying that the two guys are really only local thugs, and that because they're amateurish I shouldn't be worried? Is that it?' asked Lane. 'That's really helpful. You sure know how to comfort a guy. As a pastor you get one out of ten.'

'OK, sorry yet again,' said McCord. 'Let me do better. The fact is that you aren't in any danger, at least not yet.'

'How can you say that?' Lane asked. 'They follow me across Edinburgh and all around Fife. Someone else breaks into my house. These people, whoever they work for, are after something, and it must be something I don't know about. It can't be just the stuff about Oswald Chambers. You haven't told me everything.'

'Yes, I have,' said McCord. 'It's your analysis they're after. There is nothing else. You are the key factor in this. You are the expert who'll come up with the best idea of how and when this material will predispose the president of the United States. It doesn't matter whether that's true or not. They *think* it's true, and that's our fault. They won't touch you because they want you to finish. It's just that they don't know when you will finish, so they have to keep tabs on you.'

'What you're saying then,' said Lane, 'is that I'm in a Catch 22 situation. I'm safe as long as I don't finish, but in danger if I do finish?'

'I guess that sums it up pretty well,' said McCord, smiling broadly once again.

'Great,' said Lane. 'It was good of you to put me into this position.'

switch you on to mute. You and me, we're both beyond the pale now. Honestly, I don't know why I bother.' Mutch sighed, leaned back and stopped waving his hands. He looked at Lane. 'Anyway Davis, you didn't ask me to come here to hear me go on. What are you up to?'

Lane began to tell Mutch his story, editing it as carefully as possible. He explained that he had been given an assignment to analyze Oswald Chambers' book, but did not reveal the name of Clan Caledonia. He sketched out in broad terms the concern that the president was clearly influenced by the reading of the book, and that various parties would be interested in knowing the depth and possibilities of this influence. He said to Mutch that he thought the agency behind this assignment was the CIA, but that it was becoming clear that other parties were on the prowl. Lane told Mutch in detail about the window cleaner, the men in the white Merc and the two guys in Melvin's bus. He added the proviso that he realized he was anxious and that perhaps he was only becoming paranoid.

Mutch listened carefully for a change and then gave pursed his lips, producing a silent whistle. 'Well,' he said, 'you really have gotten yourself into something here. That's intriguing, but it must be a little scary.' Mutch seemed to studying Lane for visible signs of fear.

'Yes, it has been a little scary at times,' Lane replied. 'And what I'm getting from the book scares me as well. All this stuff about becoming intimate with God—it could be such a powerful cocktail for someone who has genuine power.'

Mutch stood up. 'Why don't we walk for a while,' he said. 'My joints get stiff if I sit too long.'

They left the exhibit and wandered slowly through dusty African carnivores.

'Do you remember what Niebuhr said about the Children of Light and the Children of Darkness?' Mutch asked.

Lane nodded. 'Yes, for the most part.'

'Well, I think that we are now surrounded by the children of darkness. There are genuinely evil people in the world, or if not evil then amoral. They have no internal set of principles or values. You open the lid and look inside many people today, and there is nothing there except a readiness to be entertained. Either that or their religion offers a reward for narrowness, mayhem and murder. I mean, this is the real world. The trouble is that we keep trying to be so damn politically correct. We don't want to offend anyone, and so we keep trying to iron out any moral and theological differences between people. We ought to confront these things head on instead of taking a politically correct steam iron to them. I mean, you know that there are some people in the Muslim camp who are anxious to kill the infidels and are ready to die at the same time. And you know that there are

'Sorry yet one more time,' said McCord. 'We didn't really know that it would turn out to be this tricky.'

'By the way, Lane said, 'I don't even know for sure that you are who you say you are. Can you provide any proof?'

'You mean you don't trust me?' asked McCord.

'Now I'm the one who is supposed to say that I'm sorry,' said Lane, 'but in the light of everything that's happened and everything you've said, why should I? Do you blame me? You could be working for MI5 or the Washington hawks or anyone else as far as I know. I phoned that number in Langley, by the way. It only puts you through to the main switchboard. It means nothing.'

'OK, you're right, and I'm glad to see you're getting smart,' replied McCord. He stood up and extracted a wallet from his back pocket and sat down again. He took several ten pound notes from the wallet and laid them on the table. 'That's for lunch,' he said. Then he fished deeply into the wallet and produced a card bound in plastic. He handed it to Lane. 'There you go,' he said.

Lane took the card and studied it. It read:

Robert V. McCord
Special Operative
Central Intelligence Agency
United States of America

'That's fine,' said Lane, 'except that it doesn't really prove anything.'

'I know,' said McCord, 'that's what I mean. Any competent person could whip this off in an hour or so. There is no way I can prove it to you. You'll just have to take my word for it. But I have kept my promise to you about the money, haven't I?'

'Sure,' said Lane, 'but all the people you've mentioned have plenty of money as well. All you've really done is confirm what I was beginning to think.'

'What's that?' McCord asked.

'That Isaiah was right.'

'Isaiah who?' said McCord.

'Isaiah the prophet,' Lane answered. 'He said that truth had fallen in the public square. He was right.'

Robert V. McCord looked vacantly at Lane and shrugged.

As they were leaving, McCord said, 'Watch how you go. Keep doing the security things you have been doing. Don't try to phone me; I'll phone you in about a week and see how you're doing.'

Lane watched McCord duck into the lane and head towards Charlotte Square. Everything was moving too fast, and everything was too precarious. Truth in the twenty-first century was like an onion, he reflected. You peeled off one layer after another, trying to get for the solid core of truth. Finally, the onion was gone, and there was nothing left.

CHAPTER 18

▼

Lane found himself unable to go home straightaway. His head was swimming and he felt curiously detached from reality. He seemed to be courting trouble no matter which way he jumped. If he finished this project he landed on a rock. If he gave it up he landed on a hard place. He had taken this thing on with only good intentions, so the present situation was totally unjust. But then that's the way the world was. He should be wise enough by now not to have to rediscover that fact. After all, it was Davis Lane who had been lecturing others about how God was limited and couldn't do everything! He wandered aimlessly along George Street, looking in the bookshops, but he couldn't focus on the titles and emerged with nothing. He studied the windows of Oddbins; there was Islay single malt on special offer, but he couldn't be bothered. He moved down to Princes Street and wandered into the music shops. There were new country and western CDs on display, but they didn't excite him. His mind seemed to be completely disengaged from the ordinary side of life.

Finally, Lane walked slowly along to Haymarket Station to catch the train to Fife. By this time, the carriages were nearly full: middle-aged men carrying briefcases and young women with children and pushchairs. Nearly everyone was on his or her mobile phone, calling to inform a partner that they were on the train and headed home. It was stupid, this wholesale use of phones to convey trivia. Still, it served to remind him painfully that even if he had had one, there was no one he could phone. Looking over the Firth of Forth from the rail bridge, he felt isolated and alone. Once back at Inverkeithing, he walked home via the way he had come, but missing out the main street. The alertness and caution he had been able to mobilize in the morning seemed to have fled. He seemed to be trapped, no matter what he did.

The house was fine. His disk and book were safe. He stood at the patio door and studied the back garden. He really ought to do some gardening. And then it hit him: 'O God,' he said to himself, 'Alison is supposed to come for dinner tonight.' He had forgotten, totally, and he had made no preparations. He would have to act fast now. The Cruiser came out of the garage, and he was glad to see it. He would need to take it to the shops regardless of the danger. It would have to be something easy to prepare this evening; there was no time for looking at recipe books and hunting for exotic ingredients.

The doorbell rang precisely at eight and Alison stood on the step looking great. She was wearing a denim skirt, which was nearly as good as jeans, and a white blouse. She was quite tanned from working in the garden. He kissed her on the cheek and ushered her into the lounge. Tonight he would entertain no thoughts of a romantic nature, even if they knocked hard on the door of his consciousness. His life was complicated enough already. He had hardly had time to get the house and meal ready, let alone mentally prepare himself.

They sat in the lounge and he went for drinks, a gin and tonic for her and a dram for himself. When he opened the cupboard door, the bottle presented itself like a long-lost friend. Luckily, there was still some gin as well. He hadn't thought about needing anything but whisky. When he returned to the lounge with the drinks, she said, 'Are you still listening to country music?' She must have seen all the CDs lying in disarray near the stereo. He should have tidied them up yesterday.

'Yes, I still like country music,' he said, 'but I haven't had much time lately to listen. Would you like to hear something?'

'Yes, please,' she said, 'but I wouldn't know what to ask for. I know so little about country.'

Lane went to his CD shelf. 'That's all right.' he said, 'you aren't the only one. Country and Western is not exactly high on the popularity list in the UK. I'll see what I can find that you might like.' Lane found Garth Brooks and put on *The Dance*. It had a nostalgic quality that he liked. He handed Alison the CD cover and she was studying it. 'Yes, I could come to like that, maybe' she said. 'Did you ever find out about the window cleaner I saw?'

'No,' he answered, 'but I'm not worried about it. He was probably a new guy in the business and he just got the wrong house.' It didn't sound a very convincing scenario to him, but it was the best he could do in the circumstances. He wished he had had more time to think about the dynamics of the evening.

'And what about your work with—who was it again? Clan somebody?'

'Yes, Clan Caledonia,' he replied, 'that's going OK.'

'You said something about Celtic the last time we talked,' Alison offered.

Lane was frantically trying to remember what he had said before. 'Oh, the Celtic connection. Not Celtic as in football, but Celtic as in a culture and the people who claim their ancestry there. It's more of a lifestyle in a way. When Christianity first came to these islands, there were two types. There was the Roman type of Christian organisation, with a great vertical hierarchy—bishops and priests and dioceses and so forth—which gradually spread up from the south in England. But the Celtic type of Christianity came over from the west, from Ireland. It was more monastic and tribal. You know about St Columba on Iona, for example. He came from Ireland, and founded a monastery with twelve other monks on Iona. They were great missionaries, going out to preach to the Picts and win them around. They didn't have this top-heavy organisation with dioceses. There were bishops, but they were under Columba. It was a much simpler way of working, and most people think it was better than the Roman type. The trouble is that the Roman type gradually won out.'

Alison was listening intently with a faint smile on her face. 'So how do you use that Celtic connection in your writing for Clan Caledonia?' she asked.

Lane wished he had never taken this line. It was getting him in deeper and deeper. 'Well, I kind of elaborate on the idea of the mystic clan that seems to sell so well today, about the Celts as being the makers of romantic songs and heroic legends in the misty glens. This goes down well in the United States. And I've got a line about these Celtic qualities being woven right into the tartans!'

Alison laughed. The little lines at the corners of her very blue eyes seemed to gather and accentuate their sparkle.

'Excuse me,' Lane said, 'but I better see to the meal. How about another drink?'

'I think if we're having wine with the meal I better not.' she said. 'I know I'm not driving, but alcohol goes right to my head. Can I do something to help?'

'Thanks, no,' Lane lied. 'It's all under control.'

In the kitchen, he thought to himself that it wasn't under control. No way. The meal wasn't even under his control, let alone his composure and identity. He had been forced into cobbling together a patchwork of white lies to explain what he was up to. He didn't feel like himself at all.

After the meal, which was better than Lane thought it might be, he suggested coffee in the lounge. Alison excused herself and Lane went into the kitchen to make the coffee. When he returned with the tray, she was standing by the patio door looking out to the garden.

'Your garden looks good,' she said.

Lane put the tray down on the coffee table and went to stand beside her. 'You're joking,' he replied. 'It's not really all that good. I haven't had much time to work in it lately. It's awful in comparison to yours.'

Alison put her hand on his arm. 'Davis, are you all right?' she asked. 'You seem distracted to me.'

Lane turned to look at her. 'I'm sorry, Alison,' he said, putting his hand in the small of her back. 'I'm not at my best—too many things happening.' Alison turned towards him and moved a little closer. She looked up at him and her grip on his arm seemed to grow stronger. Instinctively, he bent down and she reached up to meet him. He kissed her, and then her tongue was in his mouth, the tip delicately probing. He could feel one of her legs pushing gently between his knees. Her tongue became more insistent. The phone rang.

Lane drew away reluctantly. 'Sorry,' he said, 'I better answer it.' He picked up the phone and said 'Hello.' He knew who it would be.

'Hello, Davis,' she said, 'It's me, Katriona. You may remember me.'

'Katriona,' he answered, 'It's you. I was going to phone you tonight.' The blood was going to his head now, and the outside world was whirling. He watched in slow motion as Alison looked at his face and then smiled. As she walked past him towards the door, she touched his arm lightly and then waved delicately with her fingers. He nodded as she reached the door, and imagined that the sight of that little wave would stay in his head for a long time.

'Davis,' Katriona said, 'I really thought that you would phone me today. You said you would. I hung around standing by this phone for a long time and then finally made up my mind to phone you. Is there anything wrong? What's happening with you?'

"I'm fine,' Lane answered. 'It's just that I have been so busy lately and the time has just slipped by. I'm sorry.'

'What have you been doing today?' Katriona asked.

'I had Alison over for a meal, Lane said. 'I thought I had to repay her for the time I was over there.'

'Oh, that would be nice for you,' Katriona said. The telephone wires were icing up.' Is she still there?'

'No,' Lane said, 'She went home a little while ago. It's tough for her being on her own.'

'I know it is,' Katriona said, 'but I'm on my own here too. It seems like everyone else has gone away for the weekend, and I'm left holding the fort.'

'Can you not get away at all?' Lane asked.

'No way,' Katriona answered. 'I'll get called out to some emergency over the next two days. I'm stuck in my room and the sun is shining.'

'I'm sorry,' Lane replied. 'Well, if it is any comfort, I have a lot to do this weekend as well. Clan Caledonia are really pushing me.'

'I don't understand why this is going on so long,' Katriona said. 'I thought that they just wanted you to write some blurbs that could be used in their advertising. Why is it taking so long?'

'They seem to like what I'm doing and keep asking for more,' Lane replied, feeling he was getting in deeper yet again. 'The good news is that the money is coming in. By the way, I've sent you money via electronic transfer.' Maybe he could divert her a little.

'Thank you,' she said. 'I was sorry to have to ask you. I'll try to be more careful after this.'

'Look,' Lane said, 'you are there to do something different and have some fun. Stop worrying about the money thing. It's OK, there's plenty.' He hoped he had not overstated the case. What if she asked him what he was being paid for this job?

'I do wish you were here,' Katriona said, sounding more like her usual self.

'I do too,' Lane replied, suddenly realising how much this was true. He wished he were away from the tangled mess and with her in somewhere like Chichicastenango. 'But you know it isn't possible just now.'

'Yes, I know,' she said with an audible sigh. 'Anyway, it helps to talk to you. Love you.'

'And I love you,' Lane said.

It took Lane nearly an hour to clear up and put things away, but he didn't want to get up in the morning to face a sink filled with dishes and pots and pans. He undressed and went into the bathroom. After brushing his teeth, he stood for a while in front of the mirror. Who was he and what was he doing, especially tonight with Alison? If Katriona had not rung, would he have gone further? Probably not. Although she had asked Alison to check up on him, hadn't she? Maybe it would have been OK. Would Alison have gone further? Probably not, although she had noticed his state of unease. They were both just lonely, and everyone needed some human warmth from time to time. Sometime he ought to do some work on the theology of sex. The church had never really got it right about sex. It had made it into such a negative thing, even though it was an essential aspect of

God's creative effort. St Paul was probably to blame; he seemed to have a thing about women. And now the whole subject was hopelessly distorted because the media exploited it to the hilt. Someday he ought to tackle the subject, but not now. Theology was coming out of his brain. There was more than enough to be getting on with.

CHAPTER 19

▼

A more promising world marched onto the stage when Lane drew open the curtains the next morning. The sky was bright blue apart from thin strands of rose-tinted clouds layering the east. Not a ripple marked the surface of the Firth of Forth. It also looked unseasonably warm. It was a pity in a way, he thought, because he would surely be stuck in the study for most of the day. In the kitchen, with the radio news focusing yet again on party politics, Lane sat with his mug of coffee and reflected. Yesterday had been a bad day. Things had gotten out of hand, and it seemed now that only he could take charge and get some control back into life. *Grasping the nettle* is what they called it, but they never went on to talk about the sting. He would need to start thinking straight and moving faster. In the study, he sat down again with *My Utmost*. For July 26, Chambers had written that we cannot arrive at purity naturally, but that the Holy Spirit brings the absolute purity of the spirit of Christ into our lives. For August 4, he wrote that we cannot know what God's compelling purpose is for us, but that what matters is our relationship with God. And for August 15, Chambers wrote that to be born of God means that we have supernatural power to stop sinning.

It was now clearer than ever to Lane where this book was heading. It was towards the idea of the pure, sinless person who was totally engrossed in his relationship with God. This would surely prove to be the central problem of the work that he needed to highlight. In good theological thinking, a person could never be wholly sinless or pure. We may make progress in our lives, but we remain sinners, always capable of abandoning God and one another. Sin was always crouching at the door, ready to pounce. It was not only unrealistic but also dangerous to think otherwise. For a person with enormous power to embrace such an idea could prove especially dangerous. Lane knew that it was in fashion to dismiss theology as some kind of abstract gobbledegook, but in fact it portrayed the most accurate view of man possible. It avoided the typical oscillation between regarding humanity as capable of anything and humanity as fit for nothing. Lane wished that otherwise reasonable people could see this, but most didn't. It was the habit of the day to kick theology in the teeth.

It suddenly occurred to Lane that he needed a more explicit statement of faith by which to judge the whole of this book. It wasn't something that would be included in his report, but merely an analytical instrument to keep in the tool kit of his mind. It was rolling around in his brain already, but it needed to be spelled out more concretely so that he could do justice to the material. For the rest of the morning he worked to develop a simple set of affirmations that he believed expressed the essence of the Christian faith. He would set the theology of Oswald Chambers over and against this.

It was hard going. The history of the Christian church was dotted with innumerable creeds and confessions and statements of faith. They had grown out of the need to teach believers the faith or to sustain the church in times of trouble or heresy. The best that he could hope for was a very skeletal model. It would go nowhere near to expressing the richness and diversity of the theology that had been done in the last twenty centuries. How could you possibly put down some short statement that did justice to the Apostles' or the Nicene Creeds, to the thought of the early Christian Fathers, to Augustine and Anselm and Aquinas, to Calvin and Luther, to Barth and Brunner and Bultmann? It was an impossible task. Nevertheless, it had to be attempted, and it had to be adequate enough for him to use in judging the theology of *My Utmost*. After an hour of struggling, Lane began to warm to the task. The present depth of ignorance about the faith did make such an enterprise very challenging. Unless someone tried to at least hint at the majesty of the theological tapestry, most people today would never have a clue. Lane now had three pages of attempts at short statements of faith. They were all rather pathetic compared to what the great theologians could have done. He took his hands off the keyboard and sighed. It was like setting the music of the Bob Wills Cowboy Band against the symphonies of Gustav Mahler. He took the best one and reworked it. It would have to do for this job.

Jesus Christ reveals both God and man to us. In his loyalty, love, and courage he shows us what God is like and what we should be like. He is the central authority; all scripture has to be understood and assessed in relation to his life, death, and resurrection. Faith is the willingness to have an honest and lifelong conversation with God. God was in Christ offering forgiveness and reconciliation to himself, but human beings will always remain forgiven sinners, only reaching towards their maturity in Christ. The love of Christ is expressed and known through the church as the community of saints. Christians are called to interpret the world in the light of their faith and to love God and their neighbor in the world as God's creation.

Lane recognised that his little statement left out much that was important to the life of faith, but he couldn't afford to spend any more time on it. His situation was becoming too precarious. This would be sufficient for what was required. He could now go back to the book and to the notes he had made and see how adequate Oswald Chambers' theology really was. It really was time to shift into fifth gear.

CHAPTER 20

▼

Lane worked almost without stopping for the next two days. The PT Cruiser stayed in the garage. He went out only to buy a newspaper, groceries for meals, and another bottle of whisky. He kept watch on the road for the white Merc and on the coastal path for suspicious looking walkers. On the morning of the second day, he watched a white Mercedes coming slowly down the road His heart started racing again, but the car eventually turned into the warehouse parking lot. The event served to underline his anxiety. The light burned in his study for most of the day and well into the night. When he did leave the house, the book was tucked back onto the shelf and the floppy disk got lost under the globe. He saw Alison once, working in her garden and they exchanged friendly waves, but nothing more.

He received an email from Katriona:

Dear D:

I hope you are OK. I'm missing you a lot, but not just for lack of money (A joke!). The finance situation is fine now as I'm being more careful. I haven't taken any more trips.

The last few days I have been working with orphaned children. There are so many children who have either lost their partents or been abandoned. We try to find foster parents for them, but it is so heartbreaking...The problem is that there is a big trade here in adopting childfren. A number of angencies exist to promote the adoption of children by childless couples in the rich west. But a lot of the transaction seems to be about making money. Do you know that it cost over $20,000 to arrange for this? There is endless bureaucracy, and during it all the costs escalate. You watch the process going on and on and trhe people becoming more and more frustrated. And you wonder whether it will work out anyway. It is all pretty depressing.

Please email me soon and tell me what you are doing.

Love XXX

K.

Lane penned a little note to himself reminding him to reply and stuck it to the monitor. At the moment he couldn't imagine what he could honestly report. If he let on how hard he was working, she would wonder why. He jumped when the telephone rang. It was McCord.

'Hi Davis, how are you? Just thought I would touch base.'

'I'm OK,' he replied. It dawned on him that he was actually glad to talk to someone. 'I'm still working away here. I am making progress.'

'I think we ought to get together for lunch,' McCord suggested. He went on without waiting for a response. 'What about meeting at the place we met prior to the last place?'

What a convoluted question, Lane thought. But he realized that McCord was being careful not to spell out the venue.

'Yes,' he answered, 'that would be fine. I can do that.'

'What about day after tomorrow?' McCord said. 'Say at twelve-thirty?'

'OK,' Lane answered. 'See you then.' He hung up. He wasn't sure how to deal with this sudden meeting. What was on McCord's mind? The man must know that he hadn't finished his report. Did he have some new scary confession or some new problem to solve? That would be all he needed. Judging from the last few days there was no telling what the day after tomorrow would bring. Still, all he could do now was push ahead with the work and wait to find out what McCord had in store for him. He went back to the book. He was into the middle of Chambers' November now, and, praise God, the end was nearly in sight.

CHAPTER 21

▼

It was Friday, the appointed day for his meeting with McCord. Lane shaved and showered and dressed with a calm deliberateness that surprised him. A plan seemed to be taking shape in his mind, and that fact surely had to be good. He hadn't forced it; it seemed to develop during the night. His sense of confidence was growing, even though he couldn't pinpoint any reason why it should. He ate breakfast, checked for emails and then did some household duties for the next two hours. The house was badly in need of attention, and he felt that getting it in shape might boost his confidence even more. He needed to stay on top of things from now on.

At half-past eleven, Lane made his work and the house secure. He took the bike out of the garage and set off down the coastal path towards Dalgety Bay. Once again, there was no sign of suspicious cars or people. Another tanker was being towed up the Firth for Hound Point, its bridge brilliant white under the sun. A breeze from the east resisted his movement as he cycled down the path: past the quarry, up the little rise, through the gates and along the narrow beach. He was in a state of high alert, fully expecting someone to step out from the timbered hillside to bar his way, but no one did. It was amazing how you could get yourself worked up into a John Le Carre' frame of mind. Every figure could be a spy, every grove of trees a scene of ambush. The abandoned house at the end of the path seemed more vandalised than ever. Through the undergrowth he could see that all the windows had now been broken and that someone had tried to burn the wooden supports to the porch roof. But no one sprang out of the undergrowth there either. He passed through the gate at the east end of the path and cycled past the high flats at St David's Harbour. They must enjoy a great view over the Forth. He rode up Harbour Place, took the Link Road and then down towards the Metro Centre. It was busy at this time of the day, with parents on the move to collect their children from the nursery. Cars circled in the car park trying to find a space.

When Lane reached the Hope Tryst, the sun was still shining and it was actually warm. It would be possible to sit outside at the dilapidated picnic tables. Lane ordered a pint, found an empty table towards the front of the lawn and sat down. He could watch the parking lot from here.

Robert McCord's Saab pulled into the lot just after twelve-thirty, but there were two figures in the car. McCord was in the passenger's seat, being chauffeured by someone Lane had never seen before. The sight triggered a sudden sense of alarm. There had never been anyone else in this Clan Caledonia scenario, except for the blonde in tartan, and she had always seemed curiously uninvolved. Now there was someone else, a large man wearing a blue fleece and gloves. Who was he? The car approached slowly and then pulled into a space head-on to where Lane was sitting. McCord spoke briefly to the driver and then emerged slowly from the passenger seat. He was not wearing the customary smile as he came to the table, shook hands with Lane and sat down.

'What about your partner,' Lane said. 'Is he going to join us?'

'That's not my partner,' McCord answered. 'That's my minder. No, it's all right. He's got his lunch with him.'

'Why do you need a minder?' Lane asked, sitting down once again at the picnic table.

'Well,' McCord answered, 'in some situations it's helpful to have another pair of eyes and a bit of brawn.'

'You mean that unnamed parties are after you as well?' Lane said.

McCord said nothing, but gave a Gallic shrug.

Lane stood up again. 'Right, the lunch is on me today. What would you like to eat and drink?'

McCord studied the menu for a while, glancing around and beyond to the customers who were drifting in for lunch. Lane waited patiently until McCord announced his choice. Lane went into the bar, ordered the meals and returned with another pint.

'No, the thing is,' McCord said, after raising his glass, 'I seem to have a high profile at the moment, and my boss thinks that I should have the minder with me whenever I leave the office. What's worse is that they want me to go back for a meeting at Langley in order to drop out of sight for a while.'

'Oh, that's great for you,' Lane said. 'What about me? It certainly feels to me like I've got a high profile too, but I don't have a minder and I haven't been given the chance to disappear.'

'I'm sorry about that,' McCord answered. 'But the Company reckons that you aren't in any real danger yet. These other folk may be harassing you at the moment, but they need you to continue working.'

'Folk!' Lane interjected, 'I don't think of them as folk. They're thugs, and they're after me.'

McCord made no response to this, continuing where he had left off. 'The other factor is that I have several other irons in the fire that are red hot by now.' Lane expected him to say more, but he was silent, clearly studying the people who were coming into the garden for lunch. Lane thought that he seemed more ill at ease than ever before. His minder, still sitting behind the steering wheel, was unwrapping a sandwich but had his eyes focussed on his charge.

'However, the thing is,' McCord went on, 'I'll be back in one week exactly. The return flight has already been booked. They're hoping that you will have your report ready for me then, or maybe "hoping" is too weak a word. They want it soon. But let's wait and talk about it after lunch. It's getting too crowded here.'

Lane and McCord ate in near silence. McCord kept shifting in his seat and scanning the other tables. All the picnic tables were now taken and people were standing in the sunshine with drinks in hand. McCord's driver was still watching intently while carefully pouring what looked like coffee from a flask.

'Why don't we get out of here so that we can walk and talk at the same time?' Lane suggested when they had finished and paid the bill.

'Yes, I think we need to have a bit of space,' McCord replied. 'But my car will need to follow along at a discreet distance. Is there somewhere quiet to walk.'

'Let's go down towards the bay,' Lane replied.

The two men got up from the table. McCord went to his car and spoke again to the driver. They crossed the parking lot and started down the road. McCord still seemed fidgety and was quiet. His condition was beginning to spill over to Lane.

They passed the police station, crossed the road and walked along beside the park. At the end of the road they crossed over near the roundabout and started down the Wynd. The Saab was staying in sight fifty yards behind. Lane thought that this parade of two strangers closely followed by a Saab might well be the biggest thing to happen in Dalgety Bay in years.

'This is a lot better,' McCord volunteered. 'It looks as if I am always under observation these days, and it's making me jumpy.'

'You're making me jumpy,' Lane said forcefully. 'Am I being watched as well?'

'Not much doubt about that,' McCord said. 'We do know that there are at least two different parties interested in what is going on. That's the main reason I have to disappear for a week. We're certain that your phone is tapped and that they are monitoring your emails.' McCord stopped for a moment and put his hand on Lane's shoulder. 'You have to be very careful from now on.'

'Great,' Lane responded. 'So now because of this meeting today they'll think that I am turning material over to you?'

'It's possible,' said McCord. 'But that's not necessarily a bad thing. If they believe that it might take the heat off you.'

'Yeah,' said Lane. 'But if you disappear, it might also mean that they come to me looking for a copy of what I have theoretically given to you.'

'That's possible too,' said McCord. 'But not so likely.'

'Why not?' asked Lane. They were halfway down the Wynd now. Neat, well-kept gardens fronted almost every house. Lane was always impressed by how neat the gardens were in this place. His own was definitely not up to standard.

'We're sure now that the two groups monitoring you are MI5 and the WRW.'

'Who are the WRW?' Lane interjected.

'Sorry,' said McCord. 'It's our initials for the Washington Right Wingers, the Washington Hawks, or whatever you want to call them. But back to your first question: MI5 are moving very cautiously. They have to. The government has so many problems and are facing so much criticism in the wake of the war that they are walking a tightrope. If they go too far in pushing this thing and it became public, it could potentially bring the house down. So they are playing it cool. The WRW are a different story. They have real evangelical fervour. I think I told you that in this country they need to use local operatives. These guys are not very sub-tle. You know that already. They might ambush you and physically persuade you to turn material over to them. That is a possibility, I'm sorry to say. That's why I have a minder who is armed. On the other hand, they are on to a very good deal money-wise. They want to string this job out as long as they can. So while they need to pounce on you they want to do so only at the last minute. A couple more days is for them a couple more thousand pounds.'

'You are a real comfort,' said Lane, a sinking feeling in the pit of his stomach.

They had reached the corner at the bottom of the Wynd where it turned abruptly right and became Hopeward Mews. Further down was the sailing club. An untidy assortment of empty trailers and boats filled the yard. Out in the Bay yachts bobbed up and down beside their buoys. Much further out, several sails could be seen searching for wind. Lane pointed out beyond the bay to an island.

'Out there is Inchcolm Island,' he said to McCord. 'There was a priory there in the twelfth century. The monks from Inchcolm used to take worship services at St Bridget's Church. The ruins are just down the way.'

'What am I looking at across the water on the other side?' McCord asked. The two men had taken a seat on the bench near the small sandy cove.

'Most everything in Edinburgh,' said Lane. 'You can see the castle, Salisbury Crags and Arthur's Seat, and even Leith, where your office is. The most beautiful thing there in the foreground is the obsolete gas storage cylinder.'

McCord was shading his eyes in order to see better. He looked where Lane was pointing and then looked at him. 'You're pulling my leg,' he said.

'No, no,' Lane replied. 'It's so beautiful they have a preservation order on it.'

'No kidding,' said McCord. His car and minder were parked in the *cul de sac* at the end of Hopeward Mews, and the driver was still paying close attention.

'Come on,' said Lane, 'I want to show you one more thing.'

They rose from the bench and walked along the Mews. The houses here all had large windows looking over the Forth Estuary. Lane had always thought it would be a great place to live, but pricey. At the end of the road they came to the car. The minder watched and raised his hand in a half-wave.

'I don't think we should go farther,' McCord said. I can't be out of sight of this guy.'

'It's OK,' Lane said, 'only twenty yards more.'

Over the rise another stretch of the bay appeared.

'See that house?' Lane asked.

'The large, grand one?' McCord answered.

'Yes, that one,' Lane replied. 'That's the modern successor to Donibristle House. In the 16th century it was quite a place. The Earl of Moray lived here, but he was involved in a feud with the Earl of Huntly. The Earl of Moray was accused by his enemies of treason, so the king issued a warrant for his arrest. But the guy who took up the warrant and pursued him was the same man, the Earl of Huntly. Huntly arrived at Donibristle with his men and set fire to the house. Moray ran out under the cover of darkness and hid in the rocks. But the silk threads of his hood caught on fire and so Huntly caught him and killed him. But the story doesn't end there. Moray's wife was so angry that she refused to bury his body. He lay in South Leith Church, not far from your office, for six years.'

'My God,' McCord responded. 'How did they cope with the aroma?'

'I've no idea,' Lane answered. 'But I thought it was important for you to hear the story.'

'It's fascinating,' said McCord. 'but what is the point? Why are you telling me this?'

'The point is,' replied Lane, tapping McCord on the chest, 'that I don't want to wind up like Moray for the sake of Oswald Chambers. I have no desire to be crushed between the rocks of the MI5 and the WRW, never mind the CIA.'

McCord looked at Lane intently. Then for the first time that day his face broke into a grin. 'Don't worry, Davis, we'll make sure that you won't.'

'So what do you want me to do now?' Lane asked.

'Wait,' said McCord, 'let's go back to the car.'

The two men reached the car and stood by it. McCord had his hand on the door handle.

'How long will it take you to finish the work?' McCord asked.

'I can probably have the final report ready in a week to ten days,' said Lane.

'OK, that's good,' McCord said. 'I will be away for one week from tomorrow. I'll get in touch with you asap and we'll go from there. In the meantime, be careful about everything you do. Hide away or lock up your work when you go out. Assume that every conversation on the phone is overheard, and take it for granted that your emails are being read by someone else. Give every sign that you are working hard on this stuff. By the way, I should have told you before. The next instalment of your fee will be paid to your account next week, and there will be a bonus of another five thousand when you hand over your report.'

'I wasn't looking for any more money,' Lane said, 'but if that's the case then I would like it to go into my account by Friday. More importantly, I would like some protection.'

'Agreed. The money will be there,' said McCord. 'You'll be OK, Davis,' he went on, patting him on the shoulder. 'We're working on the protection thing. Now I'll have to make tracks. Can you get yourself back to the centre?'

'Yes, but while I'm happy enough to get back to the Centre,' Lane replied, 'I'm not happy about very much else.'

CHAPTER 22

▼

It was Saturday and raining, the kind of fine all-day rain which was good for the garden but bad for the soul. The dampness seeped into your spirit and pulled it down to ground level. Yet just because of the rain it would be a good day for working inside. He had lots to do and this would suit him. Lane hadn't slept well yet again, but at least it had been a creative non-sleep. It was amazing how inventive you could be in semi-conscious state. Every aspect of a problem presented itself, appearing in the kind of rich detail that was seldom possible in your wakeful state. During the night he had ranged over the whole of his dilemma and the possible solutions. By the time he got up he knew exactly how to proceed, and with that knowledge came a degree of exhilaration. After breakfast, he sat down at the desk and began to spell it out. Most of the day was spent on the computer. By nine he had had enough. He poured himself a dram and watched the news. By ten forty-five he was in bed.

On Sunday he went to church, the first time in several weeks. There weren't many in the congregation, perhaps about thirty-five or forty. But the hymns were reasonable and the sermon related well both to the lessons of the day and to the world. Lane had always believed that the preacher ought to construe the world in the light of the Word of God, and the effort that morning wasn't bad. The pace of the prayers was a little slow for him, granting him too much time to interject some random thoughts. But the content was good, and he put in a word for Katriona and himself. This congregation, like most others, was struggling. The minister had two charges to look after; money and time were always short, and the majority of people in the community indifferent. It seemed that the church everywhere in this country was caught in a swift downward spiral. As congregations and income dwindled, the less appealing became the profession of ministry. As the appeal of ministry declined, the number of applicants declined, and as the number of candidates decreased, so did their quality. And as the competence of leadership went down, so did the quality of worship and the ability to attract people into the congregation. Lane was sympathetic to anyone in the ministerial role these days; it was tough. But there wasn't much more he could do. He'd done his stint for many years, and he was still working at it in the freelance capacity; but it always seemed like a tiny drop of faith in a vast ocean of secularism.

It was easy to be critical of the church. It had made many mistakes, centering mainly on the failure to reform itself continually and on an insistence in dragging along a rigid and outdated structure. The church had much to blame itself for, but no one, even now, appreciated how strong the forces of secularism were, especially when the media purveyed it so effectively. Some future church historian, if there were any by that time, would be able to portray the situation as it really was. Lots of people were trying their best to renew the church, but it was like trying to repair the roof in the midst of a hurricane. Such thoughts coursed through his head during the last hymn. After the benediction he had a coffee and chatted to the few people he knew.

Back home there were no obvious problems. Everything was still secure. In spite of what McCord had said, he had seen no signs of danger lately: no Mercedes and no strangers on the road. He kept wondering if the various scares and alarms had been a delusion; on the surface it was just another uneventful Sunday. On the other hand…. However, he couldn't afford to go over the entire saga yet again. He had decided on a firm course of action and now certain important foundations had to be laid. Today he would have to channel all his activity on the garden because it badly needed attention. He was raking grass when Alison's face appeared over the fence.

'Hi Davis,' she called.

'Alison, how are you?'

'I'm fine,' she said, pulling off her gardening gloves. 'I thought I had this garden looking good, and then suddenly, it's full of weeds again.'

'Tell me about it,' Lane said. 'I really have to get mine under control. I've got to be away for a few days.'

'Where are you off to?' Alison asked.

'Oh, I've got to do some research for this project. Clan Caledonia are getting anxious.' Lane hated this new prevarication, but it was in Alison's best interests not to know what was happening. If his house was vulnerable then so was hers. Later on he could explain all the twists and turns of this affair.

'Alison,' he said, moving closer to the fence, 'I'm sorry about the other evening, when you came over for dinner.'

'I know,' she said. 'I'm sorry too but it's OK. I really enjoyed the evening. I haven't had a chance to thank you properly.'

Lane nodded and smiled a bit ruefully. In his mind he imagined that they were both employing "sorry" language on two different levels. 'Anyway,' Alison said, 'I'll need to get on now if the garden is ever going to get done. Have a good trip. I'll keep an eye on the house while you're away if you want.'

'Thanks,' Lane responded. 'I'd appreciate that, but if you see a strange window cleaner or anyone else around the place, don't get involved. Call the police and tell them. Take care though.' He put his hand over hers on the fence and let it linger for a moment.

By the end of the afternoon he was satisfied with what he had achieved in the garden. The grass was short and even, and most of the beds were weed-free. This would do for a while, for long enough.

He went into the house, had a shower, got dressed, and poured himself a dram. Then he sat down at the pc. It was time to contact Katriona.

Dear K:

Sorry that I haven't written much lately. I have been so busy. Went to church today. It was slim but OK> I came back and did all the garden: cut the grtass, weeded, trimmed the hedge, etc.

What's happening with you. I haven't heard a lot from you lately. Are you still doing adoptions? What about the money situation? I can send some more if required.

The project is going very slowly. I won't be able to finish when I thought I could. It's going to take another two weeks at least. However, that's just the way it is. I guess that I'm not as fast as I used to be!

Have to go now. Let me hear from you.

Love XXX

Lane re-read his email twice before pressing the 'send' button. He hoped that would do it. Then he did some exploration of web sites. Just how much could you accomplish simply by sitting at your computer and going online? It was astonishing when you really set out to exploit the possibilities.

CHAPTER 23

▼

Tuesday was a key day, in some ways the most important day in his plan. Lane took the PT Cruiser out of the garage and drove to the service station. He filled up with petrol and bought a ticket for the car wash. He didn't like using the high-pressure jet, but he needed to do highly visible things today. For once, he hoped that today he was being watched. He took his time washing the car, then checked the oil, the tyres and the water in the windscreen washer.

He left the garage and headed to the Metro Centre in the Bay. He parked and gave himself a minute in the car to think things through. He would need to do this well, a little test of his ability to obfuscate. He took a pair of trousers out of the car and went into the dry cleaners. When the attendant said, 'You can collect it Thursday', Lane replied. 'No, I can't make it on Thursday. I'll come in next week.' He took his ticket and left. He stood leisurely in front of the estate agent's window studying the properties for sale. There was one or two worth considering had he been in the market, but he wasn't. He went into the chemist's shop and bought razor blades. It was a sad day for society when you couldn't pick razor blades off the shelf. You only got a card to collect from the shelf these days. The blades had to be kept at the checkout because kids stole them from the shelf then sold them to raise money for drugs. Katriona had first alerted him about this ploy. Sometimes it seemed that the world as he knew it was disappearing. Lane left the chemist's shop and walked to the bank. Inside, he joined the queue for the teller and made a transaction. Leaving the bank he went to the newsagent, spent awhile looking at magazines and then bought a paper. He went next to the post office and bought several large manila envelopes and some stamps. He also purchased an electrical time-switch. He took his purchases back to the car and left them, then went into the supermarket. He selected, on this occasion, the large and deep trolley rather than the smaller one. In the supermarket he took his time shopping. It would need to be mostly food that could be frozen. When the trolley was overflowing he went to the checkout, groaning inwardly at the probable size of the bill. 'This is ridiculous,' he thought to himself. But it was all part of the game. He wheeled the trolley out to the parking lot and slowly loaded the groceries into the boot of the Cruiser. He locked the car and walked over to Melvin's shop.

Melvin was very busy today. There were three men waiting on the bench seats. However, the wait would suit him on this occasion. To his surprise, Melvin's old dog raised its head, got up stiffly and shook itself and then moseyed over to Lane. It sniffed his trouser leg, wagged its tail and then went back to the basket. Lane took this as more than a merely friendly canine gesture; it might be a sign. He didn't go looking for signs, but he didn't exactly ignore them either. He would have to spell out the theology of signs sometime. Melvin looked up briefly and gave him a nod of the head. Lane picked up a tattered *Scottish Field* of three years vintage and started thumbing through it. He wondered if his watchers, assuming they were there, would have the staying patience for this day.

Melvin seemed happier today. When Lane got into the chair, there was a warm greeting.

'Hello, Mr. Lane.' Melvin said, actually smiling. 'How are you?'

'I'm fine,' said Lane. 'You seem happy, Melvin. Why is that?'

'How do you want your hair cut today?' Melvin asked.

'The usual,' Lane replied. Melvin was already snipping away.

'I'm feeling good,' Melvin offered. 'Business is good and the weather is good. My team has been winning. They're now in third place.'

Melvin was working with his electric trimmer, so Lane waited for the noise to end in order to reply.

'You remember the last time I was here?' Lane asked. 'You said that there were two guys looking for me? Have you seen them again?'

'Nope,' said Melvin. 'Did they find you?'

'No,' Lane replied. 'I haven't seen them and I don't know who they were.'

'I guess if they were good friends they will find you,' Melvin offered. 'Are you still doing your crazy theology?'

'Yes,' Lane said. 'I'm still doing my crazy theology. Have you thought about what we talked about the last time?'

'A little,' Melvin said. 'But I'm used to thinking of God as being up there, you know, in the heavens. I can't think of him as being down here and in the world.'

'Why not?' Lane asked.

'He's God, you know, and It can be kind of grotty down here,' Melvin answered. 'Too much trouble in the world. I wouldn't like him to be beside me in the stands on a Saturday night, with all that bad language.'

'He's used to that, Melvin,' Lane said. 'Remember that he was here in the person of Jesus. He knows what it's like. He always stands beside you wherever you are.'

'I suppose so,' Melvin said, ploughing a new furrow in the back of Lane's neck. 'It's just so different.'

'I know,' Lane said. 'But think of God as the ground under your feet, or the ground of your being. He's the source of things. He's under and around us all the time.'

'Yeah,' said Melvin, now finishing the top of Lane's head. 'I'll try to think about that.'

Melvin held up the mirror so that Lane could study the back of his head.

'That's fine,' he said. 'By the way, if these guys come around again looking for me, tell them that I've been working very hard. But say to them that I told you I would be finishing what I'm working on in a couple of weeks.'

Melvin was removing the cloth from Lane's head and looking at him quizzically. He handed Lane a tissue to brush the hair from his face.

'But Melvin,' Lane went on, wiping his forehead, 'don't tell them that I know they are looking for me. Let's let them have their surprise.'

'OK, whatever you say, Mr. Lane,' said Melvin. 'How can they find you?'

'As you said, Melvin,' Lane answered, 'I'm sure that they'll manage.'

On his way out Lane walked over to the corner of the bus and gave Melvin's dog a couple of strokes. It raised its head briefly and then nestled it in between its paws once more.

At home again, Lane parked in the driveway and took his time unloading the groceries and carrying them into the house. The freezer was full once again. He opened the garage door and put the PT Cruiser inside. Locking it up, he patted it on the roof and said 'Cheerio. Be careful.' He felt a sense of accomplishment. Things were progressing well.

It was dull the next morning, leaden skies and grey waters. He was up by six-thirty and at the desk by seven. The report had to be in its final form by the end of the afternoon. He needed to state his final conclusions about Oswald Chambers and *My Utmost for His Highest* very carefully. The right form of words had to be meticulously crafted. What he wrote here could affect people. At least he hoped it would. How well he expressed things here did matter. By three he was printing. He panicked when the printer ink ran out, then remembered that he had a replacement cartridge in the cupboard. Lucky, because he couldn't afford to encounter problems at this stage. While the printer laboured, Lane gathered the other things he needed and arranged them neatly in his briefcase.

At four Lane phoned Clan Caledonia. It was, he was sure, the blonde who answered. He heard the same flat tones: 'Clan Caledonia. Good afternoon, may I help you?' she asked.

'Hello, it's Davis Lane,' he said. 'The freelance theologian. Do you remember me?' He mentally pictured her reading *Hello* at the other end of the line. He was distracting her once again.

'Oh, yes, Mr. Lane,' she said, indifferently.

'May I speak to Mr. McCord?' he asked.

'I'm sorry,' she answered. 'Mr. McCord is away on a business trip.'

'Right,' Lane said. 'I'd like to leave a message for him. It is quite important though and I want to make sure he gets it.'

'Of course,' she said. 'I'll pass it on as soon as he gets back.'

'Can you tell Mr. McCord that I'm not finished yet but that I should be done with my work at the end of next week, either Thursday or Friday. Ask him to give me a ring when he gets back.'

'That's fine,' she said. 'I'll pass that on, Mr. Lane.'

'OK, thank you, but don't forget now,' Lane said, and hung up. Another piece of the plan put in place.

At five he climbed the loft ladder to find the holdall. He packed everything he could think of, but he knew that it wasn't done as well as Katriona would have done it. It had been raining most of the afternoon. He ran though the rain to check the back door of the garage and the gate to the garden. At seven he took out a ready-made meal from the freezer and put it in the oven. While it was heating he made one last check of the briefcase and the holdall and set them out in the hallway. He installed the time switch and plugged in the desk light in the study, setting the switch to stay on until twelve every night. At eight he ate his meal; it was actually not too bad. It must be his frame of mind. At half-past eight he turned on the TV and watched a mindless reality program while waiting for the news and the worldwide weather forecast. After switching off the television, he poured himself a dram and put a CD into the player. He listened to LeAnn Rimes all the way though. By eleven he was in bed. But sleep did not come easily; too many wheels were turning. He kept wondering if he had remembered to do everything that was required for his plan to work. If he hadn't he could be in deep, deep trouble.

CHAPTER 24

▼

Lane was up by six. He lad laid everything out the night before, so by six-twenty he was dressed. It was still raining as he closed the window, but that was OK. Today the rain might actually work for him. He had some cornflakes and a coffee and threw the rest of the carton of milk out. He went around the house twice, setting the heating and checking the windows and doors. At seven-twenty Lane picked up his holdall and briefcase and slipped out the back door. He walked up the lane and turned into the main road, then through the parking lot, along the old railway track and down the slope to Inverkeithing Station. The 0742 was on time and surprisingly full. He hadn't appreciated how many people commuted into the city at this time in the morning. And almost without exception once again they were on their mobile phones. Who were they phoning at this time in the morning? After the train had crossed the bridge, the guard came round and Lane bought a single to South Gyle. If anything would throw them it would be this. At South Gyle he got out and walked the path along the tracks towards the main Glasgow road, passing the sports centre and the playing fields. The only people about were those who had dogs to walk. Mercifully, the rain began to ease off. On Glasgow Road he waited until a free cab came along. It took a while, but he had anticipated this, allowing himself plenty of time.

At Edinburgh Airport, Lane checked in. The holdall could go into baggage, but the briefcase would stay with him at every point. The holdall was checked all the way through to his destination. The girl at the desk handed back his passport and boarding pass and smiled. 'Have a nice holiday,' she said. He hadn't thought of it exactly like that until now, but why not? It was certainly an "escape" of some kind. Just thinking about the word gave him a real lift.

He went through security without any problem and into the domestic lounge. In the duty free shop there was no Lagavulin. He had counted on that and felt let down, but perhaps at Heathrow. Lane bought a newspaper and sat down. He couldn't relax yet. Did he have everything he needed? Had he made things secure at home?

The lounge at London's Heathrow Airport was very crowded. Lane hunted until he found enough space on the seats for him and his briefcase. He opened the case and set out his materials in an ordered fashion. He had three copies of his full report on *My Utmost for His Highest*. He took the time to read through it once again:

A THEOLOGICAL CRITIQUE OF *MY UTMOST FOR HIS HIGHEST*

In the book *My Utmost for His Highest*, Oswald Chambers provides the reader with a devotional reading for each day of the year. Each reading bears a phrase or sentence as a title and has a scriptural reference. These readings were compiled after Chambers' death by Mr. Chambers' wife from her shorthand notes, and were first published in England in 1927. It could reasonably be argued that had Chambers written the book as a whole it might have enjoyed a greater unity and more systematic nature. However, the book is used today by a great many people as a daily devotional aid, and a website exists to enable loyal Oswald fans to study his work and communicate with each other about it. For this reason, some critical appraisal of the work is probably important, over and above the stated purpose of my involvement.

I have attempted to do a short critique of this work, not from a strictly academic perspective—for the work does not purport to be a systematic theology—but from a point of view sensitive to how the work might influence the typical reader. So I shall consider how Chambers uses scripture, what major theses occur in his thinking, and how his theology squares with the traditional Christian affirmations.

Hermeneutics. Chambers interprets scripture in an inconsistent manner. He does not employ a literal interpretation, which is neither possible nor intelligent in any event. (Those who urge literalism conveniently neglect certain hard passages and ignore other passages which contradict each other). On the other hand, he does not employ any obvious standard with which he might interpret or give weight to the rest of scripture. He appears to make no distinction between the Old and the New Testaments. One might argue that he has an "Opportunistic" approach to hermeneutics, for he plucks passages willy-nilly from the Bible in order to provide a theological basis for a particular idea that he wishes to promote. At times he flatly contradicts scripture. For example, in the devotion for December 16, Chambers says that to wrestle with

God in prayer is unscriptural. Yet in the passage concerned (Genesis 32:24-25), Jacob's wrestling with God must surely be regarded as a positive event. Jacob learns something of the nature of his divine opponent and, having revealed his name, is then blessed by God. Chambers would not, however, be able to agree with this interpretation because of his stress upon total surrender and obedience to God. "Wrestling with God" would be regarded by Chambers as disobedience. This is merely one example of a highly problematic interpretation of scripture.

Doctrinal Affirmations. At the very centre of Chambers' theology is the doctrine of salvation, made possible by the atonement of Jesus Christ. The death of Jesus, rather than the resurrection, is central to Chambers. Most theologians regard the resurrection as the key affirmation, as does the New Testament itself. For Oswald, complete surrender to God leads to intimacy with him. The discipline of remaining intimate with God leads to sanctification, or personal holiness. The Holy Spirit, working in the believer, effects a new creation. The qualities of Jesus are imparted to the believer: patience, love, faith, holiness, purity and godliness. The believer then has the power to stop sinning and lead a life of soundness, order, and holiness. Through a disciplined faith, the believer may then look forward to a time when nothing of the old life remains: no old gloomy outlook, no old attitude towards all things, no lust, no self-interest, and no sensitivity towards ridicule from others. The characteristics of the old or natural life are sacrificed: the believer's personal plans and ambitions, and his own thoughts, insights and understandings. The notion that the believer ceases to sin altogether and leads a holy life without a vestige of his former life remaining is not something recognized by the New Testament.

Ethics. From a moral point of view, the believer's intimacy with God means that he is enabled to make perfect moral decisions. Chambers can actually say that we 'are the will of God'. The characteristic of love is spontaneity. The believer's conscience will be in agreement with Jesus in every situation. Chambers' ethics are closely tied to his doctrine of God. God is in everything and controls everything. He ordains every event; in the life of the saint there is no such thing as chance. Eating and drinking, walking and talking are all ordained by God. God especially ordains the crises that come to people. In such crises there is the opportunity to respond to him. The believer's role when others suffer from a crisis is to offer intercessory prayer, which is the real business of life. The believer, according to Oswald, is not to be sympathetic to the struggles and sufferings of the other; rather he might well *pray that his difficulty will grow even ten times stronger, until no power on earth or in hell could hold him away from Jesus Christ.*

Chambers' view of the believer's relationship with others is best considered under the rubric of "missionary work". We are to reproduce our own kind spiritually! We are to exhibit ourselves as trophies of God's grace. The goal of missionary work is not the elevation of people, or their education, or their needs, but their discipleship to Christ. God's goal is to produce saints. But the believer must be careful not to be "tarnished" through his bodily life with others.

The implications of this theology for the doctrine of creation are profound. The believer is not to attempt to better the world in any way; he is only to win souls for God. So while the believer is in the world he really takes no responsibility for it. Indeed, Chambers' view of the world is quite negative; it is gloomy, drab, and problematic. So his theology always telescopes back into itself; while Chambers says that the believer is not to withdraw from the world, he must by necessity always retreat from it into prayer and personal holiness.

Chambers has little to say about worship and the church. Worship takes place in the context of the believer's private relationship with God. The problem of the church, he says, is that it is too concerned with its organizational affairs. The believer is to build up the Body of Christ by completely surrendering himself to Christ. So the believer has a unilateral relationship with others; he wins others to Christ, but never receives anything from them, except perhaps the possibility of being tarnished by them.

Conclusions. In conclusion, we must say that *My Utmost for His Highest* has a very badly flawed doctrine of God and of Jesus Christ, a wholly inadequate doctrine of creation and sin, and a defective understanding of the nature of humanity. The most positive thing I can find in this work is Chambers' emphasis on the disciplined life of the believer. It is possible to see that if a person were to have an ill-disciplined life or destructive habits or addictions, then this book might well be of benefit. Otherwise, however, it cannot be said to express sound Christian theology.

Of particular concern is Chambers' idea of morality or ethics. The idea that the believer achieves such intimacy with God that he is able in his moral actions to express the will of God perfectly is very dangerous. He speaks about a *feeling of restraint* brought on by a check in the spirit. But how likely is that for one who feels intimate with God? Ethical activity ought always to involve the most careful intelligent analysis and thought in the service of love. This is because, however sanctified we are, we are also always sinners. *Were a person of substantial authority and power to follow Chambers' counsel without appropriate restraint, the results for the society and world could be genuinely disastrous.*

By Davis Lane, Freelance Theologian

To this report Lane attached a letter, which he also read once again:

Central Intelligence Agency
Langley, Virginia
FAO: Robert McCord

Dear Sirs:

As you already know, I was approached in Edinburgh, Scotland by one of your agents, Mr. Robert McCord of Clan Caledonia Exports, to make a theological analysis of Oswald Chambers' book *My Utmost for His Highest*. At least, Mr. McCord indicated that he was one of your operatives and showed me some credentials to that effect. He indicated that the idea behind this study was to explore or foresee the implications of the disciplined use of this work by the President of the United States, a practice that has been widely reported.

I have carried out this study and have been remunerated for it by the agency (presumably). I enclose my report for your information. I hope that you will give it your immediate attention.

As you will see from my report, there is a considerable danger lurking within the pages of Oswald's work, assuming of course that it is taken seriously. The most obvious danger lies in the area of ethics. The thesis is presented that as the believer moves towards intimacy with God, he also moves towards sanctification, or personal holiness. It is further stated that in such a state the believer perfectly does the will of God. Indeed, *he is the will of God*. The implication is that no systematic thought need be given to moral activity, nor does thought need be given to the consequences of action. I am confident that you will appreciate the dangers of this position were the action to be performed by a person of great authority and power. I think on this matter I need say no more. I trust that you will find this analysis helpful.

Incidentally, Mr. McCord indicated that other agencies or groups might also be interested in gaining access to this report. I have had personal experience of such interest. I take it that you will be aware of this. Please give my regards to Robert McCord and express my apologies that I could not wait to see him in person in Edinburgh.

Thank you for your assistance.

Yours sincerely,

Davis Lane
Freelance Theologian

Lane attached the letter to the report, placed it in an envelope addressed to the CIA and stamped it. He next took up a second letter and scanned it once again:

The Director
MI5
PO Box 3255
London SW1P 1AE

Dear Sir or Madam:

Please find an enclosed analysis and critique on a book by Oswald Chambers entitled *My Utmost for His Highest*. I was contracted to do this project by a person who is purportedly an agent of the CIA in Edinburgh. The book is important because it forms a significant part of the staple diet of the President of the United States and as such may well exercise considerable influence upon him.

As you are no doubt aware, the relationship between the British Prime Minister and the President is very close. The theory presented to me (which I accept absolutely) is that the future policies/actions of the President are bound to have a significant impact upon the Prime Minister and thus upon the United Kingdom. I encourage you to read this report carefully, for you will undoubtedly see the concerns that the Prime Minister might need to be informed of or guarded against. I have already been remunerated for my work, and so I am happy to share it with you free of charge.

By the way, if the two guys in the white Mercedes who tailed me and broke into my house were your agents, please say cheerio to them. If they were not your agents, then it might be a good idea to discover for whom they were working.

Thank you for your assistance.

Yours sincerely,

Davis Lane
Freelance Theologian

Once again Lane attached the letter to the report, placed it in an envelope, sealed and stamped it. He picked up the final letter he had written and spent a longer period of time re-reading it:

The President of the United States of America
The White House
Washington, D.C.

Dear Mr. President:

I don't know whether this will ever reach you personally or not. Never having written to the president before, I am woefully ignorant of the means by which contact can be made. I can only hope that whoever sorts the enormous amount of mail addressed to you appreciates the importance of what I have enclosed and passes it on.

I was asked to analyse and prepare a theological report on the book *My Utmost for His Highest*, by Oswald Chambers. I know that you use this book in your daily devotionals. And that is precisely why, Sir, I was asked to do this job. There are apparently a number of people/agencies who would like to know how your dedication to this work might affect your policies and your actions as the most powerful person in the world. I'm sorry that I can't be more specific about exactly who is interested or who asked me to do this work. It could be the CIA. It could be MI5. It could even by the neo-conservative group who are reputed to wield great power in Washington. I have tried to think this through, but the layers of obfuscation are so many and devious that they have left me in a fog. For a number of weeks now I have wondered if I were paranoid, always looking over my shoulder, seeing shadows, and hearing footsteps behind me wherever I go.

However, I can assure you that I do not think this has affected the quality of the theological analysis that is in the enclosed report. I am impressed, Sir, by the disciplined way that you employ this book in your daily life of faith. I can see why it is so important to you. I too feel that the discipline we must exercise as Christians is vital. It is the only way that we come to have the virtues of faith, hope, and love.

However, there are certain issues in the book about which I believe you must be informed. You will find these clearly indicated in the report. The most serious one is that of moral activity. Oswald Chambers has made a very serious mistake in his doctrines of sin and man. He sees man, as he draws near to God and is sanctified, as moving away from being a sinner. He believes that intimacy, through the power of the Spirit, gives us an ability perfectly to express the will of God. He can even say that *we are the will of God*. Thus, no careful, logical thought about the consequences of action is required. *Mr. President, that is completely wrong. We never*

*are completely the will of God. We are always sinners. And while we grow
in grace towards our maturity in Christ, we never quite make it.* Anyone
who reads St Paul will see this. According to him, he cannot do what he
wants to do; and he does the very thing that he hates.

So no matter how we feel spiritually, moral action always requires the
most careful, logical, and informed consideration. And unlike the advice
of Oswald Chambers, seeking the counsel of others is crucial, especially
the advice of those who have no military or political axe to grind. I hum-
bly submit, Mr. President, that as the most powerful man in the world, you
have an obligation, and a specifically Christian obligation, to think
through your actions in the most careful way possible. Oswald Chambers
does not seem to care much about the world, but God does, Mr. President. It is his creation and he loves it. You own immense power to shape
the world, and I am hopeful that you will use it wisely.

Yours sincerely,

Davis Lane
Freelance Theologian

Lane put down the letter and sighed audibly. It wasn't perfect. There was so
much more that needed to be said. But if he went on at greater length it would
probably be discarded at first sight. Moreover, the whole thing seemed arrogant;
who was he to write to the president? Nevertheless, he had already made up his
mind and had set the plan in action, so he would stick to it. He attached the final
copy of the report to the letter, placed it in the last addressed envelope, and
stamped it. He closed the briefcase, picked himself up off the couch and walked
through the lounge until he found the large red pillar-box. With one more, long
look at the envelopes, he popped them through the slot. Watching them drop, he
already felt lighter. Then he went to look for some malt.

On the Virgin flight headed for Guatemala City, Davis Lane unfastened his
seat belt and pushed the button to recline his seat. He settled back, closed his eyes
and said a little internal prayer: *Thank you, God, for this day and for getting me
though the last period of time. Thank you for Katriona. Keep her safe. Let some good
come from what I have done. Amen.*

When the stewardess came round and asked him if he wanted a pre-dinner
drink he replied, 'I don't suppose you have a Lagavulin, do you?'

'I'm sorry, sir,' she said, rummaging through her drawer of miniatures, 'I
don't. But would a Johnny Walker do?'

'A Johnny Walker will be fine,' Lane answered.

He pulled down his tray and carefully set the miniature, the glass and the water down. He extracted his portable CD player from the seat pocket and put on the earphones. From his portable CD carrier he pulled out a CD and put it is the player and shut the lid. He poured out the Johnny Walker, added some water and raised the glass.

Katriona would be so surprised to see him standing at her door, assuming of course that he could find her flat. He tried to picture her jaw dropping in astonishment. He hoped that she would be able to take a few days to go to Chichicastenango. He was ready for that. 'Cheers' he said, nodding the glass. He pressed the 'Play' button and Willie Nelson came into his head once again:

...on the road again...
Goin' places that I've never been....

978-0-595-36911-9
0-595-36911-1